MASTER CROOK'S
CRIME ACADEMY

BURGLARY FOR BEGINNERS
and ROBBERY FOR RASCALS

TERRY DEARY

For Lisa Edwards

Scholastic Children's Books,
Euston House, 24 Eversholt Street,
London NW1 1DB, UK
A division of Scholastic Ltd
London ~ New York ~ Toronto ~ Sydney ~ Auckland
Mexico City ~ New Delhi ~ Hong Kong

Burglary for Beginners first published by Scholastic Ltd., 2009
Robbery for Rascals first published by Scholastic Ltd., 2009
This edition published by Scholastic Ltd., 2019

Text © Terry Deary, 2009
Illustration © John Kelly, 2009

The right of Terry Deary and John Kelly to be identified as the author and
illustrator of this work has been asserted by them.

ISBN 978 1407 19562 9

Printed and bound in the UK by CPI Group Ltd, Croydon, CR0 4YY

2 4 6 8 10 9 7 5 3 1

This is a work of fiction. Names, characters, places, incidents and dialogues
are products of the author's imagination or are used fictitiously. Any
resemblance to actual people, living or dead, events or locales is entirely
coincidental.

Papers used by Scholastic Children's Books are made from wood grown in
sustainable forests.

www.scholastic.co.uk

BURGLARY FOR BEGINNERS

Contents

ROBBERY FOR RASCALS

Contents

MASTER CROOK'S

CRIME ACADEMY

BURGLARY FOR BEGINNERS

Before word

YOU MAY NOT REMEMBER 1837. YOU ARE PROBABLY A BIT TOO YOUNG. YOU MAY BE ONE OF THOSE SAD PEOPLE WHO HAVE BEEN FORCED TO GO TO SCHOOL – A PUNISHMENT FAR WORSE THAN FIVE YEARS IN DARLHAM GAOL IF YOU ASK ME! BUT, IF YOU HAVE BEEN TO SCHOOL, YOUR HISTORY TEACHER MAY HAVE TOLD YOU THAT 1837 WAS THE YEAR THE OLD QUEEN CAME TO THE THRONE.[1] THOSE ARE THE SORTS OF THINGS THE HISTORY BOOKS WILL TELL YOU. BUT THE STORY I HAVE TO TELL YOU IS NOT SO WELL KNOWN. THAT 'S BECAUSE IT ALL HAPPENED IN A QUAINT, COASTAL TOWN IN A NORTHERN CORNER OF THE COUNTRY. WHAT HAPPENED THERE WAS SENSATIONAL. SENSATIONAL. IF IT HAD HAPPENED IN THE CAPITAL OF OUR COUNTRY THEN THE HISTORY BOOKS WOULD BE FULL OF IT.

BUT IT DIDN'T. IT HAPPENED IN THE POOR LITTLE, MUDDY LITTLE, COLD LITTLE, WIND-WRACKED, WAVE-WASHED, SMOKE-

---

1 It was quite a large throne because she had a large bottom, of course. In fact she was a short but wide young lady at the time. She grew wider as years passed. Several people tried to shoot her, as you know. They all missed. How they missed such a w-i-d-e target I'll never know.

CHOKED, RAT-RIDDLED, SOUR-SMELLING LITTLE TOWN OF WILDPOOL. A TOWN THAT TIME FORGOT. A MIDDEN THAT'S HIDDEN.[2]

SO THE STORY IS ALMOST FORGOTTEN. YOU CAN FIND PARTS OF THIS TALE IN THE PAGES OF OLD NEWSPAPERS, A FEW FADED DIARIES AND TOWN COUNCIL REPORTS, THE ODD LETTER AND SCRAPS OF DUSTY PAPER.

IT WOULD TAKE A LONG TIME FOR YOU TO GATHER THE PIECES AND MAKE SENSE OF THE STORY, SO I HAVE DONE IT FOR YOU. I HAVE SPENT A LIFETIME GATHERING THE FACTS AND THE PAPERS SO I CAN SHARE THE STORY WITH YOU.

IT IS THE STORY OF A GREAT PLAGUE OF CRIME THAT SWEPT OVER WILDPOOL LIKE ONE OF THE WINTER WAVES ON WILDPOOL BEACH SWEEPS OVER THE PIER. A CRIME WAVE![3]

AND 1837 WAS AN ODD TIME TO SEE SUCH A SURGE OF CRIME. YOUR HISTORY TEACHER WILL HAVE TOLD YOU THAT IN THE 1830S THE FAMOUS ROBERT PEEL INVENTED THE POLICE FORCE TO STAMP OUT CRIME IN THE COUNTRY.

2 I like that phrase, don't you? Of course you youngsters may not know what a midden is. In these days of dustcarts and flushing toilets no one has a midden any more. It was a rubbish tip made up of ashes and all the disgusting things that nobody wanted. Just like Wildpool in fact.

3 Another little phrase I have invented and that I like a lot. I think it could catch on. But I am interrupting. "Again!" You cry. Sorry. I will try to control myself. Forgive me if I burst out into twittering notes like a skylark. It is the excitement, you know.

SO, WHY (YOU ASK) DID CRIME IN WILDPOOL GET WORSE, NOT BETTER WHEN THE FIRST POLICE BEGAN TO PATROL?

I WILL TELL YOU, I REPLY. THAT IS WHAT MY STORY AIMS TO DO.

WHO AM I? AND WHY AM I SO INTERESTED IN THE WILDPOOL WAVE OF CRIME? YOU ASK (YOU DO ASK A LOT OF QUESTIONS, DON'T YOU?).

I WILL NOT TELL YOU WHO I AM. ALL I WILL SAY IS THIS: I SAW WHAT HAPPENED BECAUSE I WAS THERE AT THE TIME. I MAY APPEAR IN THE PAGES OF THIS SUPERIOR STORY . . . BUT YOU WILL NOT KNOW IT IS ME.

WHY? YOU ASK. WHY DO I WISH TO STAY HIDDEN IN MY OWN TALE? WELL, SOME OF THE THINGS I DID WERE OUTSIDE THE LAW. I AM NOT ASHAMED OF WHAT I DID. BUT I AM TOO OLD TO GO TO JAIL FOR CRIMES THAT HAPPENED OVER SIXTY YEARS AGO.

READ ON FOR A CHRONICLE OF CRIME THAT WILL CHILL YOU COLDER THAN THE EAST WIND THAT WHISTLED THROUGH THE WILDPOOL STREETS THAT WINTER.

A TALE OF TERROR, OF TREASURE AND OF TWISTLE.

MR X[4]

22 JANUARY 1901

---

4 No, Mr X is not my real name. In fact I may not even be a Mr. Perhaps I am a Miss or a Mrs, a Lady or a Lord! But I promised to stop cutting in with these needless notes, didn't I? So don't read this one.

Chapter 1

GRAVE WORDS
OF GRANNY

"Never forget," Mrs Smith said. "Never forget what your granny said with her last breath."

"What was that, Mum?" a boy with ragged black hair breathed.

"Your granny looked up from her deathbed—"

"I thought she was run over by a muck cart," the boy interrupted.

"She was, Smiff."[5]

---

5 Yes, that is right. The boy was called Smiff Smith. His mother had to register his name in the church when he was born. When the clerk asked the boy's name she said, "Smith" . . . as you would! The clerk wrote it down as his FIRST name AND managed to spell it wrong . . . he didn't want to cross it out or change it because he felt a bit of a prawn. So Smiff Smith was given his name.

BIRTH REGISTRATION 1827

NAME: Smiff Smith,
FATHER: Silas Smith,
OCCUPATION "Sea Captain (deceased)"
MOTHER: Belinda Smith,
OCCUPATION "Coal worker"
PLACE OF BIRTH: 71 Low Street, Wildpool.

The woman went damp around the eyes. "We carried her into the house and laid her on the kitchen table," Mrs Smith said and sniffed sadly.

"So it wasn't a death bed?"

Mrs Smith was starting to look a bit cross and her lips went thin and white. "All right. Your granny looked up from her death table and said, 'Never forget, Belinda . . . You can never have too many mop buckets!'"

"Too many mop buckets? What's that supposed to mean?" the boy asked.

Mrs Smith shrugged. "Dunno, Smiff. She died before she could tell us. Oh, how I cried!"

"Because Granny was dead?" He asked gently.

"No, because we couldn't afford a funeral!" she snapped.

"What did you do?"

Mrs Smith shrugged. "It was the muck cart that ran her down, remember, so it was the muck cart that carried her away to the town dump. She didn't mind. She was dead."

Smiff peered at his mum through the sputtering light of the mutton-fat candle.

"Are you lying, Mum?"

She smiled her twisted smile. "All our family tell lies, Smiff. It's what we do best. You know that. But I've never forgotten your granny's last words and I've never been short of mop buckets. Go out and get me one, son."

Smiff sighed. The coal fire was glowing warm. The street cobbles outside were covered in ice and he had no shoes to his name.[6]

---

6 That's an odd thing to say. No shoes to his "name". Why don't people say, "I had no shoes to my feet"? Or "No shoes to my shoe-cupboard"? I don't know. I thought you might know. Excuse me for asking.

Smiff was thin as a rat's tail and had no fat to keep out the cold from his bones.

"Aw, Mum!" he groaned.

Mrs Smith grabbed him by the collar and hissed at him through her yellow teeth. "You wouldn't refuse a dying granny's last wish, would you?"

"No, Mum," he sighed. The boy wrapped a blanket around his shoulders, took one last loving look at the fire and pushed the door open.

The wind was sharper than a butcher's knife, slicing through his blanket and thin shirt. "Why doesn't Mum ever send me out to steal something useful," he muttered through his chattering teeth.[7]

"Something like a warm, woollen coat?" But she never did.

He stepped over the horse droppings and crossed the road by the green-glowing gas

7 The teeth were chattering to each other as there was no one else in the street to chatter to. But at least they had each other. It is very lonely having no one to chatter to. Granny had a lonely tooth before she died. A single tooth in the middle of her mouth. She was the first woman in the country to have central eating.

lamp. The wind stabbed at him as he climbed up the steep hill of Low Street. At the top he turned towards the High Street. He hurried past dark alleys. A clumsy dust-cart driver almost ran him down . . . Smiff thought the man may have been trying to. "Mum would send me to my funeral on your cart!" he shouted at the man but the clattering hooves and rattling of wheels on the cold cobbles drowned his voice.

At last he reached the row of shops. The apothecary with glowing glass globes of red, blue and yellow liquid cast their rainbow light on the pavement. Smiff hurried past. The wizened wizard who owned the shop was as scary as a rat with rabies and twice as ugly.

He trotted on past the grocer, the greengrocer and the baker, the hat shop and the pawnbroker till he reached the hardware shop with its tin pots and clothes pegs, china cups and pewter mugs. Smiff slipped through a maze of ropes and riddles, candles and cart-grease, buckets and brooms, knives and forks, hammers and handsaws.

The boy picked up a hammer. He picked up a mop bucket. He looked around. He felt something was watching him. There was no one there . . . or so he thought.

He smashed the hammer against the side of the mop bucket then marched up to the counter.

A thin old man stood there, as grey as the boy's blanket, and peered at him. "My mother is mad," Smiff said.

"Then see a doctor," the old man told him in his creaking-floorboard voice.

"I mean angry-mad. You sold her this bucket and it has a dent in the side!" Smiff showed him the dent he had just made. "She wants a new one, or else!"

"Else?"

"Else she'll come down here with her wet mop and shove it up your nose . . . she says!"

"Better take a new one, son," the shop owner sighed. "I'll lose the money it cost me," he said, shaking his head.

Smiff almost felt sorry for him. But when the old man stepped from behind the counter the boy saw he was wearing boots. He must be rich, Smiff decided.

The boy left the shop with a shining new mop bucket wrapped in brown paper.

A man in a shabby top hat stood on the street corner. His gooseberry-green eyes glowed in the gas-light. His fingers were fine as twigs on a vine. They rippled when he talked.

As Smiff walked past him he clapped his hands softly. "Well done, my little thief," he said. "You almost got away with that."

The boy shivered and it wasn't with the cold. "Are you a watchman?" he asked.

The man smiled and ivory teeth glowed under his thick, dark moustache. "No. Not the watch. I am Samuel Dreep, a teacher."

"I've heard about teachers," Smiff shuddered. "They take rich children into schools and beat them till they learn."

"I don't work for that sort of school," Dreep laughed. "I will walk with you back to your house in Low Street and explain. . ."

"You know where I live?"

"Oh, yes, young Smiff. We know a lot about you. You are the sort of young man who will do very well in our new school."

"But Mum taught me how to read and do letters," Smiff boasted.

"Ah, no," Dreep said shaking his head. The two walked down Low Street and the man trod carefully so his leather boots didn't slip on the icy cobbles. "I am a teacher at the famous Master Crook's Crime Academy and I believe I can help you. Come with me."

"Master Crook's Crime Academy? I've never heard of it."

"It's secret . . . but the name is famous in certain parts of the city. Let me show you."

He pulled out a neat piece of cardboard with a printed picture of a fine house. The boy held it under the light of a flaring gas lamp to read it.

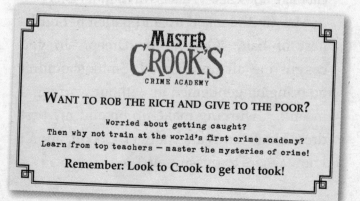

MASTER CROOK'S
CRIME ACADEMY

WANT TO ROB THE RICH AND GIVE TO THE POOR?

Worried about getting caught?
Then why not train at the world's first crime academy?
Learn from top teachers — master the mysteries of crime!

Remember: Look to Crook to get not took!

"Get not took?" Smiff blinked.

"Get not caught . . . don't get caught," Dreep shrugged. "But 'get not took' sounds better. It's poetry."

Smiff shook his head.

"My mum needs her mop bucket," he said and hurried on.

"She has enough mop buckets," the tall man cried.

"You can never have too many mop buckets," Smiff said. "Never!"

He led the way through the battered front door into the dark hallway of his house. It smelled of dead cats and cabbage. "Hi, Mum! We have a visitor," he said and hurried into the warmth of the living room that smelled of dead cabbage and cats. "This is Mr Samuel Dreep."

Mrs Smith looked up and patted her bird's nest of hair. "Ooooh! Mr Dreep, sir, you caught me all unprepared. Smiff shouldn't go bringing gentlemen in without warning. I mean . . . with my make-up on and my best dress I look ten years younger. Ooooh, I don't know where to put myself."

Samuel Dreep stepped forward and took Mrs Smith's hand. He raised it to his lips and kissed the grubby paw. "Mrs Smith, you already look ten years younger."

"Ten years younger than what?"

"Ten years younger than Granny," Smiff muttered.

"Your son is so talented," Dreep went on. "A thief as skilful as a cat in a cream factory."

"He is that," Mrs Smith beamed. "Taught him myself."

"I am here to make you an offer. Send him to Master Crook's Crime Academy and he will make you a nice little income for your old age."

"Old age?" she said sharply.

"And your young age! We will train your son in the art of crime. No more stealing trifles like mop buckets. He will bring you diamonds to sparkle like your bright eyes, gold to fill your shining silk purse and dresses of satin to show off your fine figure!"

"Ooooh! Mr Dreep," she giggled like a girl being tickled in a feather factory. "You are naughty." She turned to her son. "Here, Smiff, fill the mop bucket from the pump in the yard and boil some water over the fire. I'm sure Mr Dreep would like a cup of tea. "

"Aw, Mum! I just got warm again."

"No tea for me," Dreep put in quickly.[8]

"I am from Master Crook's Crime Academy and I want to invite young Smiff to join. I can make him a master of the art of crime. The school opens its doors for the first time tomorrow. Your son can be one of the first pupils. He can make it to the very top."

Dreep pulled a square of paper from inside his coat and slipped it on to the table in front of Mrs Smith. Smiff looked at it. Mrs Smith looked at it.

"We call it a school-home contract," Dreep explained.

"Ooooh! There now, Smiff!" she sighed.

---

8 Can you blame him? I mean, Mr Dreep liked tea – we all do. But to know it was boiled in a mop bucket is not a nice thought. Mop buckets are very useful . . . as we shall see . . . and you can never have too many. But please don't use them to make tea.

CRIME ACADEMY

I Belinda Smith *hereby agree to enrol my son* Smiff Smith *in the school known as Master Crook's Crime Academy.*

I also swear on my granny's teeth:

- not to tell anyone about my child's school or snitch to the law
- to make sure s/he sticks to the school rules at all times and doesn't skive or play truant
- to make sure s/he does their homework
- to support the teachers even if they give him/her a smack round the ear for being cheeky
- to make sure he has the school uniform and a good pair of boots.

The school agrees to:

- give you half of what your child makes from his/her crimes
- pay for your child's funeral if s/he has an accident while doing a dangerous job OR gets caught and is hanged.

Signed
Belinda Smith[9]

---

9 You will notice this document is signed by Mrs Smith. That 's because it is one of the genuine papers I have collected over the years. How did I get my hands on it? That would be telling.

Mrs Smith laughed, "That looks very fair to me. Very fair."

"I don't like that bit about being caught and hanged, Mum," Smiff frowned.

"It's all right, son!" She grinned her yellow-toothed grin. "The school will pay. I know you are worried about your dear mum having to fork out for a funeral. No need. Look. It's here on the paper." She ruffled his black hair playfully.

"No, Mum, paying for my funeral isn't what I was worried about," Smiff said angrily.

"Look, son, what are the chances of you being caught? Eh? The town watch are a bunch of old men that have more noses between them than teeth. They couldn't catch a dead dog if it ran into the town jail and gave itself up."

"Now then, Mrs Smith," Samuel Dreep said softly. "I think there is one small matter I have to tell you about. It's only fair."

"Small matter?"

"The small matter of the town watchmen."

"What about them?"

"They won't be around for much longer," Dreep said and stroked his moustache carefully.

"All the better for Smiff!" Mum shrugged.

"No. What I mean is they are about to be replaced. There is a new sort of law officer about to walk the streets of Wildpool."

"Ooooh! Hear that, Smiff? A new sort of law officer about to walk the streets of Wildpool," his mother said and poked him in the shoulder.

"Yes, Mum, I'm not deaf. I suppose these new officers will be sharper than the old watchmen, will they?" Smiff groaned. "I suppose there'll be more chance of me dangling on the end of a hangman's rope?"

"It depends who gets the officers' jobs," Dreep said with a soft smile.

"I still don't like the sound of these new officers. What are they called?"

"They are called police," the tall man said.

"Sound horrible." The boy sighed. "Don't sign that paper yet, Mum."

Mrs Smith waved it happily in the

candlelight. "Too late, son, too late. It's all done. You start at Master Crook's Crime Academy tomorrow."

"Thanks, Mum," Smiff said bitterly. "Thanks."

"That's all right, son," the woman said and wrapped an arm around his thin shoulders. "Master Crook will make sure those nasty Please Men don't get you. Isn't that right, Mr Dreep?"

"We're working on it right now," Dreep said. "Right now. . ."

Chapter 2

TRUNCHEONS OF FIRE

Wildpool town hall was the pride of the town and Wildpool's mayor was the pride of . . . well, the pride of himself.

Tall and handsome, elegant and awesome . . . I mean the town hall, of course, not the mayor. Smoke stained and with twiddly knobs struck on . . . I mean the town hall, not the mayor. A neat little beard, a pair of gold-rimmed spectacles and a fine black suit . . . I mean the mayor, not the town hall.

The mayor was Sir Oswald Twistle. A legend in his own mind. A man as tall as any gnome, as mean as a wasp with toothache and as rich as a conquering king. He had the mighty brain of a turnip . . . as large as a turnip but not quite so clever.

Sir Oswald said his family arrived with William the Conqueror back in 1066. Sadly they decided to stay.

He used his wealth to bribe and buy people and of course they made him mayor. It was worth every golden coin to Twistle to stand there on the town-hall stage and speak to his adoring people in front of his adoring wife.

"People of Wildpool!" he cried. There were at least twelve people crowding into the council chamber that was big enough to hold a hundred. "People of Wildpool!" he repeated. His voice was a little squeaky and didn't sound quite so grand as he imagined. Mayor Twistle turned to his wife who sat on a velvet chair behind him. "I just said 'people of Wildpool' twice, dear," he muttered.

His wife, Arabella Twistle, had written the speech for him. She always wrote his speeches. She was a large woman. She was a very large woman. Her dress of pale green silk would have made a fine sail for one of the ships in Wildpool harbour. Her face would have made an even finer figurehead on the bow.[10]

"Yes, Ossie, dear. You have to say it twice to grab your listeners by the ear. Make them sit up and listen!"

"They are standing up," the mayor said.

Under the hard white mask of make-up, Arabella Twistle's face began to glow as pink as the lace bonnet that framed her fat face. A face as hard as the diamonds that lay on her large, white chest. "Read it, Oswald. Read it. Trust me. I am the best writer in Wildpool – probably the best writer in the whole country. Read it!"

The mayor gave a single nod and turned back to the crowd of eleven . . . one had slipped out to the toilet. "People of Wildpool!" he cried.

"You already said that," a blind beggar sniffed. He was only in there to get out of the cold.

10 You know what a figurehead is, don't you? One of those wooden women who were stuck to the front of sailing ships back in those days. They stared ahead and dared the seas to do their worst. Arabella Twistle's wooden face would not have dared the seas . . . it would have scared the seas. Waves would have run and hidden under the nearest island.

"People of Wildpool!" the mayor repeated.

"Four times," the beggar sighed.

"Today is a day that will go down in the annals of Wildpool history!" Mayor Twistle read.

"What's annals?" someone cut in.

Lady Arabella leaned forward and spat, "Books. History books."

"Right!"

"This very day the streets of Wildpool will be safe for all decent people to walk abroad. To tread the precious cobbles of our glorious town, knowing that we are safe from the dangers of thieves, rogues, varlets and beggars."

"You what?" said the beggar.

Twistle read on. "People of Wildpool! I, Oswald Twistle, your mayor, am proud and honoured to announce that we will have a new force of law and order walking the streets. A police force!"

"What's that then?" one of the twelve asked. (Yes, the twelfth one was back from the toilet.)

"Men in uniform will patrol the streets and guard our persons, guard our homes, guard our factories and guard our wealth!"

"I haven't got any wealth," the blind beggar snapped.

Sir Oswald Twistle ignored him. "A new law allows us to have one police officer for every thousand people in the town. Wildpool has two thousand people. So we will be guarded not by one lone police officer, but by two . . . or three if we count the inspector in charge."

Arabella Twistle leaned forward to explain. "Though of course the inspector will not be walking the streets. He will be at the station."

"Waiting for a train?" the beggar asked.

"The police station, not the railway station," Lady Twistle hissed. "A new building at the side of the town jail. Very handy for locking up people like you . . . so watch it, mate."

"Here don't you go threatening me!" the beggar croaked. "I've not done nothing wrong!"

"My police will find something if you don't shut your ugly mouth," her ladyship spat.

"Ugly? That's the cat calling the pottle black. You're as ugly as—"

"Stop!" Mayor Twistle shouted. "Stop it. Let me finish my speech." Silence fell over the mighty crowd. The mayor shook his paper and read. "I will sweep the streets of Wildpool clean of the filth that fouls its gutters. I will give us a town to be proud of. A town . . . wipe a tear from your eye . . . eh?" He looked back at his wife.

"No-o!" she moaned. "You do that . . . wipe a tear away . . . you don't say it!"

"Sorry, dear." He turned to face his public. "A town . . . sniffle . . . where our children can play happily in the parks of green. . ."

"They'll have to watch out for the dogs' droppings," a mother muttered.

"Where we can walk safely in the streets. . ."

"Not to mention the horse droppings," her friend added.

"Tonight it is my great honour, joy and delight to introduce to you . . . the men who will guard us like the angels that they are!" Mayor Twistle waved a little hand to the door at the side of the chamber.

The door creaked open a crack. "Now?" a voice whispered.

Twistle nodded. "Constable Liddle and Constable Larch!"

The old oak door was flung open and two men stepped out shyly. They blinked in the bright gaslight that flooded over the stage. Constable Liddle was as old as the oak that made the door and thinner than one of its twigs. His wispy white moustache trailed like a sad dog's tail.

"He looks just like the old watchman but dressed in a new uniform," the woman whispered to her neighbour.

"That's cos he is the old watchman dressed in a new uniform," her friend replied.

"Oh, good! I thought me eyes were playing tricks!"

Liddle shuffled along and stood next to the stout, red-faced, piggy-eyed man that was Constable Larch. They fumbled with the ebony sticks at their belt. The sticks had gold lettering that said "WP" and a coat of arms with a blue shield held up by two ducks and topped by a goat rearing up.[11] (The coat of arms of the Twistle family, of course.)

11 You can still see one of these truncheons in Wildpool Museum today. It is inside a locked glass case. Not only does the case keep the dust off it but it also stops school children taking hold of it and using it to play rounders. The trouble is there is a human skull in the next case that would make a perfect ball. Museums would be much more fun if they allowed truncheon-and-skull rounder games, wouldn't they?

THE FIRST WILDPOOL POLICE TRUNCHEON USED BY
PC LARCH (OR MAYBE PC LIDDLE) WHO WERE THE FIRST
POLICE IN WILDPOOL. THE STAINS ON THE END COULD
BE THE BRAINS OF A CRIMINAL CRACKED BY PC LIDDLE
(OR MAYBE PC LARCH). THE SKULL CAN BE SEEN IN THE
NEXT CASE. OR THE STAINS COULD BE PORRIDGE THAT
WAS STIRRED BY LARCH AND LIDDLE (OR MAYBE LIDDLE
AND LARCH) FOR THEIR BREAKFAST. WILDPOOL MUSEUM
SALUTES THESE HEROES.

They wore matching uniforms of navy blue
with silver buttons. Of course the police in the
capital had worn uniforms like this for five
years but Lady Twistle drew her own design
for the boys in blue of Wildpool.

COLLAR — TOUGH LEATHER TO STOP THE OFFICER
BEING CHOKED BY GARROTTERS

SHOULDERS — NUMBERS (SO THEY DON'T GET THE WRONG
JACKET AND SO THE PUBLIC KNOW WHO'S WHO . . . OR WHO'S
TWO! JUST MY LITTLE JOKE)

POCKETS — FOR NOTEBOOK AND PENCIL TO MAKE NOTES.
NOTEBOOKS NOT TO BE USED FOR DOODLING. POCKETS NOT TO
BE USED FOR CHEESE SANDWICHES

TROUSERS — LOOSE SO THE OF CER CAN RUN LIKE A HARE
(WELL IF HARES WORE TROUSERS THEY WOULD RUN LIKE A
WILDPOOL PC. MAYBE)

UNDERWEAR — A LADY DOES NOT DRAW MEN'S UNDERWEAR

BOOTS — FOR WALKING TEN MILES A NIGHT. HEAVY IRON TOE-CAPS TO KICK CATS OUT OF THE WAY (AND IN CASE THE OFFICER DROPS HIS TRUNCHEON ON HIS TOES)

HAT — TALL TOP HAT, MADE FROM TOUGH LEATHER TO PROTECT THE MEN FROM STICKS AND STONES AND COSHES

SHIRT — WHITE. OF CERS MUST BE CLEAN AND CHANGE SHIRT AT LEAST ONCE A WEEK. (TWICE A WEEK IN SUMMER WHEN THEY GET REALLY SWEATY AND SMELLY)

BADGE — THE COAT OF ARMS OF THE TWISTLE FAMILY

JACKET — NAVY BLUE WOOL, NOT TOO THICK (COS WE WANT THEM TO KEEP MOVING TO KEEP WARM!) SILVER BUTTONS (BUT NOT REAL SILVER)

BELT — BLACK LEATHER WITH CLEVER LITTLE HOOKS TO HANG TRUNCHEON, HANDCUFFS, DARK LANTERN AND RATTLE[12]

SOCKS — NAVY WOOL. TWO PAIRS SO THEY CAN CHANGE THEM ONCE A MONTH

Wildpool's new boys in blue were ready to rattle and roll down the steep streets and awful alleys, catching criminals and righting wrongs, beating beggars and locking up law-breakers.

12 Of course in the twentieth century you expect to hear a policeman blowing his whistle to call for help and tell the world there is a peace-breaker on the prowl. But those old policemen used wooden rattles to clatter out their warnings. If they lost their truncheons they could give the criminal a battle with the rattle! You can't do that with a whistle, can you? Rattles are a sad loss if you ask me.

If PCs Liddle and Larch looked scared stiff it was only because they didn't like standing on the stage being stared at by huge crowds (of ten or more). Once they were rambling down the roads they'd be fine.

Probably.

The constables had stepped out of a small room leading off from the council chamber. If we could look through the old oak door we would see a man in there. A large man. A very l-a-r-g-e man, not much wider than the door or heavier than a carthorse. He called himself Police Inspector Beadle.

Police Inspector Beadle did not wear a uniform. Police Inspector Beadle's fat face was not a face the people of Wildpool would see on the streets. That was the job of Larch and Liddle.

Police Inspector Beadle wore a plain suit of dark grey, a white shirt with a starched collar that was almost lost in the rolls of fat around his neck.

He tapped the pages of the report in front of him.

WILDPOOL POLICE FORCE
REPORT

DATE: 3 January 1837
        PC Septimus Liddle (PC 0I) and
        PC Archibald Larch
        PC 02) signed on today.
        Liddle is thin, ancient and not very
        bright.
        Larch is heavy, slow and as bright as a
        dark lantern.
        They will do the job we need.

        POLICE INSPECTOR BEADLE

Police Inspector Beadle smiled softly, folded the report and slipped it inside his jacket.

In the council chamber the mayor, who was only just taller than a gnome, stretched out an arm and pointed to the door. "What are you waiting for? Get out there and fight crime!"

Lady Twistle tugged angrily at his coat tails and rustled a piece of paper under his nose. "Read this, Ossie, the way I told you."

"Sorry, dear." Sir Oswald Twistle cleared his throat and squeaked the words. "Go forth into the jaws of terror, my brave lads!" Then he read the epic poem his wife had written for this great day.

Fight for the right
By day and by night.
Go forth, and we bless you,
Though criminals test you.
Though they chase you with guns,
We know you won't run.
Though they chase you with knives,
We know you won't hide.
Go forth the world wide
We are there by your side . . .
. . . so to speak.

He added, "Carry your truncheons like flaming torches of justice. Bring light to the darkness of our savage streets. Go, our heroes, go!"

The crowd burst out in applause. Mayor Twistle looked pleased and his wife almost cracked her make-up with her smile. "I think they like me," he whispered.

"I think they liked my speech," she huffed.

"Oh, yes dear. Sigh. Of course, dear. But one day they may like me. One day."

Constable Liddle turned his head stiffly in the hard leather collar and muttered under his moustache. "Chase us with guns? Police Inspector Beadle never said nothing about guns!"

Larch spoke out of the side of his fat mouth. "Police Inspector Beadle caught us stealing pennies from the little match-seller's tray. He said we'd go to prison if we didn't sign up for the police."

"Suppose so," sighed Liddle. "So let's get out there and catch some criminals."

"It's cold out there," Larch moaned.

"It's colder in Darlham Gaol cells."

"You're right. Let's get out there."

Shoulder-to-shoulder the two constables faced the crowd. They bent their knees and spoke with one voice, as Inspector Beadle had taught them. "Evening all!" Then they stepped from the stage and marched through the crowd who parted to form a sort of guard of honour. Someone opened the door and an icy blast of air struck their faces. The two men were almost in step as they marched down the High Street.

"So let me get this right," Liddle said slowly. "The mayor wants us to set fire to our truncheons and use them as flaming torches?"

"No, Liddle. I don't think he meant us to do it really."

"That's good. That's really good."

"Why?"

"Cos I haven't any matches."

"Ah."

The green gas lamps glowed and lit the streets below them like a necklace of diamonds. Yellow light flared in the shipyards by the river. Hammers clanked on the new, steel steamship that would be one of the first in the world. It was called "The Pride of Wildpool".[13]

In the distance, across the river to the north, the fairground by the seashore lay dark and empty. On the higher ground to the south the mansions of the rich folk glittered smug and snug.

The railway trucks clattered and clanked while Locomotive No. 2 sparked and steamed. Coal trucks rattled down to the piers and tipped their black load into the waiting collier ships.[14]

It was never quiet in Wildpool.

The constables looked around. "So? Where do we start?"

"We could walk down Low Street to the river?" Larch said.

Liddle gasped. "You're joking! That place is full of criminals! You won't catch me going down there at night!"

"Ah."

And so on that historic night the new Wildpool Police Force set out to fight for the right by day and by night.

But very carefully, of course.

13 I won't tell you how it got that name.

14 The piers were called 'drops' – if they had loaded lemons instead of coal I suppose they'd be lemon drops.

Chapter 3

SACKS OF SWAG

Snow was falling as Smiff stepped out of his house the next morning.[15]
His mother had done as Samuel Dreep asked and bought Smiff a new pair of boots. He even wore a pair of warm woollen socks.

Smiff marched up the steep hill, past the terrace of pitifully poor houses that made up Low Street. Many had boards across the windows to keep out the draughts. Glass cost too much for the poor of Wildpool, even though there was a glass factory just at the first bend of the Wildpool river.

Samuel Dreep waited for Smiff at the top of the hill, and was wrapped in a fine scarf of

---

15 Well, you didn't think the snow would be rising, did you?

red and white stripes. He wore black leather gloves and that shabby top hat as tall as a stove pipe. His boots were of the finest leather. Almost a gentleman, in fact.

"Good morning, Smiff," he said with a smile. "I hope you slept well?"

"A bit cold," Smiff shuddered.

"Soon you and your mother will be able to afford some good blankets to get her through to spring," Dreep promised, then spread his thin fingers wide. "If you do well at school, of course. But you will eat and sleep at the school."

Dreep turned and led the way through the snow-blown streets. Men and women hurried to work, heads down and collars turned up. The snow was white, the soot-stained walls of the houses, factories and shops were black, the faces of the people were grey. It looked like one of those moving pictures you see at the cinema these days . . . though cameras had not been invented back in 1837, as you know.

Dogs jogged in search of rats to eat, but the rats were hiding warm in their holes too deep for dogs to dig them out.

"Good morning officers!" Dreep called across the mud-slushed, horse-clopped, cartwheel-slopped cobbles.

Smiff looked up sharply. Two men in navy uniforms with high hats shivered in the shelter of the soap-factory wall. "Mornin' all!" they said with a stiff-jointed bend of the knees.

"May I take this chance to wish you the very best of luck with your new jobs, Constables."

Liddle and Larch gave frozen-lipped smiles. "Thank you sir."

"Who are they?" Smiff hissed.

"The enemy," Dreep said softly.

Dreep and Smiff soon arrived at a rambling and shambling house. It had once been a fine town house of a ship owner. But Wildpool grew. The huddle of houses on the riverside spread up the hill and streets like Low Street were thrown up.[16]

Soon the ship owner could see shoddy slums at the corner of his road. He could smell

16 When I say "thrown up" I don't mean vomited. They were thrown together in a hurry and were slums as soon as they were finished. They were slimy and smelly. So maybe I do mean like vomit.

the corpse-scented homes. He moved out to the hill beyond the south edge of the town. The part where all his rich friends lived.

His old house had been saved from the hammers of the wreckers. Now, a sign hung on the green gates.

MASTER CROOK'S

CRIME ACADEMY

TUITION FOR THE CHILDREN OF THE POOR TO HELP THEM STAY OUT OF PRISON.

And that was true, in a way! Master Crook would teach them so well they would never be caught – they would stay out of prison. (Darlham Gaol was a hateful place ten miles to the south. You wouldn't want to spend time in there.)

Behind the green academy gate was a small garden with a winter-withered tree and a tall, black-brick house with a newly painted door – a red door that matched Dreep's scarf.

Dreep took out a key and unlocked the door. "We usually keep the door locked ... there are a lot of thieves about," he said, looking hard at Smiff.

"Very funny, I think not," Smiff said.

They stepped into a hall with a floor that shone with polish and stamped the light snow off their boots on to a mat.

The house had been a school for just one day but already it smelled like a school.[17]

The doors were painted cream and the walls were painted a muddy shade of yellow. A new noticeboard had been nailed to the wall. It only had one notice on it.

17 You may be unlucky enough to go to school. In that case you will know the smell I mean. All schools smell like a mix of wooden desks, teachers' mouldering breath and chalk dust – always chalk dust. Even after the last child has escaped from the last school they will still smell the same.

SCHOOL RULES

PUPILS MUST ...

1 RUN IN YE CORRIDORS AT ALL TIMES
2 BE LATE FOR YE LESSONS
3 DISOBEY YE TEACHERS
4 WRITE ON YE SCHOOL WALLS
5 SHOUT YE OUT ALOUD
6 CHEAT IN YE TESTS
7 EAT IN YE CLASS
8 PICK YE NOSE AND EAT YE IT
9 DAMAGE YE BOOKS OR CARVE YE NAMES ON YE DESKS.

BUT:
10 PUPILS MUST NOT PICK ON OTHER PUPILS. NO MATTER HOW WEEDY AND WORTHLESS A CLASSMATE LOOKS THEY ALL HAVE A PLACE AT MASTER CROOK'S. BE WARNED. BULLY NOT OR YE SHALL BE BULLIED.

"Huh!" Smiff sniffed. "Master Crook likes to say 'ye'."

"Yes, ye does," Dreep agreed.

Smiff stepped into a large room with a fine, high ceiling. Plaster angels with plaster horns to their lips looked down. A small coal fire burned in an iron fireplace and warmed the room. The windows looked out across the river to the north side of the town and the snow-capped hills.

There were five desks in the room and they faced a blackboard. But there was just one pupil sitting there. A girl as thin as Smiff but with curly fair hair and blue eyes like a doll. But she was dressed like Smiff – trousers and shirt, waistcoat and jacket, all a grim grey colour. She glared at Smiff (grimly).

"Meet Alice White," Dreep said. "Your first partner in crime."

"Pleased to meet—" Smiff began.

Alice cut in, "He doesn't look much of a criminal to me. I've seen deadlier dog droppings than him."

"Thank you, Alice, but Smiff is a skilled young thief," Dreep began to explain.

"Hah! Who says? You says?" the girl snorted. "So if he is so-o skilled, what's he doing here, eh? If he is so-o-o-o skilled he has nothing to learn. He's wasting his so-o-o-o-o-o skilled time, isn't he?"

Dreep pulled off his gloves and red scarf and laid them on a table at the front. "He just thinks too small," he explained. "We want to help him – and you – rob the rich to feed the poor."

"Or rob the rich and get hanged for it . . . if skinny Smiff is as useless as he looks," the girl said and gave a sudden, savage, small-toothed smile.

"Alice. . ." Dreep said quietly. "You are not much of a big-time criminal yourself, are you?"

"No, well, yes, well, I made a living—"

Dreep cut in and said, "Alice was trying the Lucifer Dodge, weren't you?"

"Huh! So what? So what?"

"What's that?" Smiff asked.

The tall teacher stroked his fine moustache and explained. "A child takes a tray full of matches to sell on the street. As a rich gent walks past she spills them as if he's knocked them out of her hand. She scrabbles on the

47

ground to pick them up and howls her little heart out. If the gent doesn't give her money then other people passing by may cough up a coin or two."

"So she gets paid for matches without selling them?" Smiff said.

"That's right. In fact she sells them over and over again. She gets her little friends to gather up the matches and try it again . . . and again."

"I make shillings a day," she argued.

"And we will teach you to make sovereigns a day," Dreep promised.

Alice opened her mouth to argue but Dreep went on, "Now meet your first teacher," he said and walked to a door that seemed to lead into the next room.

"Master Crook?" Smiff gasped.

"Ha! No, Master Crook is too busy finding new teachers and new pupils, making plans and setting up dodges. No, we have been very lucky. We have found one of the best burglars in the whole country." Dreep threw the door open and cried, like a showman in a circus ring. "Step forward, Bert!"

A round man rolled into the room. A man older than Smiff's mother with a face full of stubble ... not at all like Smiff's mother. He had a white jersey with black stripes around it. [18]

He wore a black mask over his eyes but with eyeholes cut out so he could see. He carried a sack with "Swag" written on it. He looked a bit like a burglar really.

"I'm a burglar," Bert said proudly.[19]

"I didn't think you were a jockey," Alice sneered. "Too fat by half."

"Potatoes," Bert sighed. "They was my downfall. I love potatoes. But they make you fat if you eat too many."

"Lor' you must eat a sack a day to get like that," the blonde girl giggled.

Dreep coughed gently. "Can we get on with the lesson, please, Alice?"

"S'pose so," she shrugged.

But once Bert the Burglar started talking

18 Or it could have been a black jersey with white stripes around it. In the tricky world of crime it could have been white with black OR black with white. That sort of thing is SURE to confuse the police. Remember this when you next plan to burgle a bungalow or filch from a flat.

19 I hate it when people say "I told you so". But I did. I TOLD you so!

Alice forgot her malice and listened like a cat at a mouse-hole.

Bert told them some of the rules that saw him safely through a life of crime and Alice licked her lips at the thought of how she could copy.

"But that was the old days," Bert said. "You have a new problem. We just had to dodge the old night-watch patrols. Watchmen was just ordinary family men taking turns at watching the streets. Easy to dodge them – or bribe them to set you free if you got caught. You have to deal with some new law officers." The burglar lowered his voice and it shook a little. "Police!"

"I've seen them!" Smiff cried.

"There you go! They have their eye on you even before you've started!" Bert moaned. "New laws need new tricks. Now, how are we going to deal with this force of highly trained, tough and ruthless men who can't be bribed?"

"Easy," Alice said. "There's only two of them. Send them off to some other part of town while you burgle a mile away."

Dreep patted his hands together. "Well done, Alice. I can see you are going to be a star pupil."

"I was going to say that," Smiff sniffed.

"Yeah, well you didn't, rat-face," Alice snapped. "I said it. I am going to be the brains in this team. You can carry the loot."

Smiff didn't have an answer to that so he gave it, ". . .!"

Bert the Burglar went on for an hour and gave them all his top tips. "Don't go in the front door, of course. You'll be seen in the light of the street. Slip round the back gate. Up the garden and in the back door."

"What if it's locked?" Smiff asked.

"I was going to say that," Alice objected.

"Yeah, well you didn't, cat-face," Smiff smirked.

"I will teach you how to open locks with a skeleton key," Bert promised. "And Master Crook has the most amazing plan. A scheme to tell you which houses will be empty."

"Great!" Smiff grinned.

"Of course you have to make sure. . ."

Bert began. But Dreep heard the clock chime twelve and stopped him. Big mistake.[20]

"After lunch," Dreep said. He led the way to a large kitchen at the back of the school where hot soup was bubbling away on an open fire and a fresh white loaf of bread stood on the table.

Smiff had never seen so much food and he ate till he was stuffed. "Pig," Alice muttered as she sipped at her soup like a lady.

After a pot of tea they went back to the classroom and spent an hour learning to pick locks. Then Bert went on to list some of the things they should be looking for.

MASTER CROOK'S CRIME ACADEMY
BURGLAR BERT'S TOP TIPS

Small and preshus is best - one jewel is wurf a fowzand copper pans ... and it is a lot eezier to carry.

---

20 You will see why later.

- **Metal** is for meltin - you cant sell gold cannlesticks but you can melt em down and sell the gold they is made of. same with silver orneements.

- **Cutlery** is all right - nives, fawks and spoons sell well. But they rattle about when you carry them off. Carefull what you pinch.

- **China** is pretty uzeless - it chips and breaks and is hard to sell.

- **Cash** - well, coppers and sovrins are nice if you see some lying around.

Posh people use bank notes these days. But you cant spend em. No one would take a bank note off a poor person like you. Notes is trubble.

- **Clothes** - we all like a bit a silk or some nice sheets or blankerts. But they can be hard to hide. Have you seem them hoops those ladys have in their skirts?

- **Candels** - Wax candels, not the mutton fat ones that smell when they burn. Eezy to sell is candels. stick em in.

• **Paintins** – hard to carry, imposserbull to sell cos they is ooneek. Try selling one and its a short cut to jail. Forget em – even the pretty puppy pitchers that you love.

* last – don't get greadie. Fill up yer bag and leg it out as fast as yer can. Take it from one what nose.

"I hope you are a better burglar than you are a speller!" Alice jeered.

"Meaning. That's all that matters," Bert argued. "You get my meaning, don't yer? So button your cheeky little lip and take a telling."

Alice pouted. She pushed out her bottom lip – but she didn't have a button to button it with. In fact she didn't have a button-hole in the other lip either. So she pouted instead.

Now it's all very well being cheeky to your teacher. Teachers can take it. That is what they get paid to do. The problem is you may upset your teacher a bit.

An upset teacher is a bad teacher.

And Burglar Bert was a bad teacher that afternoon. He taught the two students almost everything he knew . . . but not quite everything. He forgot something.[21] The thing he was going to tell them when the lunch break clock had chimed.

If Alice hadn't been cheeky about his spelling he may have remembered. But she was, and he didn't.

That's why Alice and Smiff make a terrible mistake. A mistake that might cost them their short little lives.

But Smiff didn't see the flaw in the plan. Even smart little, curly-haired, blue-eyed, big-brained Alice didn't spot it.

Oh dear. Oh dear, oh dear, oh dear!

21 You don't need me to tell you what Bert forgot to tell them, do you? I mean, you are so clever you have already spotted it.

Chapter 4
SPEAKING SPIRITS

The two new students at Master Crook's Crime Academy went back to the school kitchen. They shared a pot of tea and scones.

"Is this real butter?" Smiff gasped.

"Yes, and real plum jam," Alice added, spreading the sticky purple mess thickly over her scone.

"What's jam?" the boy asked.

"Mmf-mmf nn Mmmmf!" Alice answered with a mouth full of scone.[22]

---

22 As you know this means "Try it and see". Please don't speak with your mouth full like this charmless child just did. You could spit crumbs all over your feet. Passing pigeons could then swoop down and attack those crumbs, pecking your feet till you bled to death. Remember: speaking with your mouth full kills.

Smiff tried it and drooled at the sweetness. "Ooooh! That's nice!" he said. He'd never tasted jam before, not even when his father was at home and bringing in money. Dripping fat – the grease off mutton chops – was the richest thing Smiff ever got to spread on his bread.

Samuel Dreep nodded as he stood by the fire, polishing his hat. "That's the sort of food you can have in your house if you work hard. Tender beef, pork pies, fruit jellies and sugared candies. Work hard and you'll be fat as a cat in a mouse-filled house."

"When do we start?" Smiff asked.

"As soon as you've finished tea," Dreep said and his green eyes glowed in the amber light of the fire. "Today is the first day of the rest of your life," he said.

"And the last day if we get caught," Smiff sniffed. "So where do we start?"

"In the Apollo music hall," the man told him.

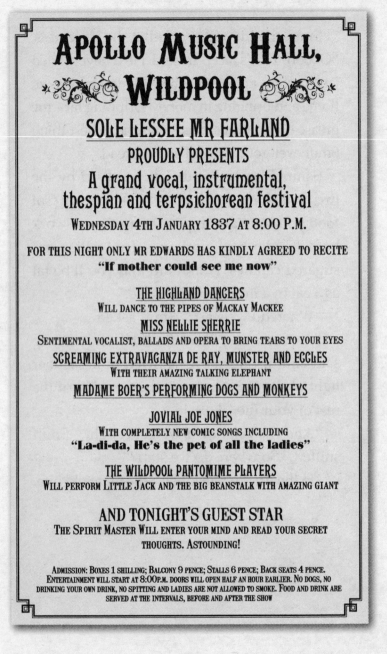

APOLLO MUSIC HALL, WILDPOOL

SOLE LESSEE MR FARLAND

PROUDLY PRESENTS

A grand vocal, instrumental, thespian and terpsichorean festival

WEDNESDAY 4TH JANUARY 1837 AT 8:00 P.M.

FOR THIS NIGHT ONLY MR EDWARDS HAS KINDLY AGREED TO RECITE
"If mother could see me now"

THE HIGHLAND DANCERS
WILL DANCE TO THE PIPES OF MACKAY MACKEE

MISS NELLIE SHERRIE
SENTIMENTAL VOCALIST, BALLADS AND OPERA TO BRING TEARS TO YOUR EYES

SCREAMING EXTRAVAGANZA DE RAY, MUNSTER AND ECCLES
WITH THEIR AMAZING TALKING ELEPHANT

MADAME BOER'S PERFORMING DOGS AND MONKEYS

JOVIAL JOE JONES
WITH COMPLETELY NEW COMIC SONGS INCLUDING
"La-di-da, He's the pet of all the ladies"

THE WILDPOOL PANTOMIME PLAYERS
WILL PERFORM LITTLE JACK AND THE BIG BEANSTALK WITH AMAZING GIANT

AND TONIGHT'S GUEST STAR
THE SPIRIT MASTER WILL ENTER YOUR MIND AND READ YOUR SECRET THOUGHTS. ASTOUNDING!

ADMISSION: BOXES 1 SHILLING; BALCONY 9 PENCE; STALLS 6 PENCE; BACK SEATS 4 PENCE.
ENTERTAINMENT WILL START AT 8:00P.M. DOORS WILL OPEN HALF AN HOUR EARLIER. NO DOGS, NO
DRINKING YOUR OWN DRINK, NO SPITTING AND LADIES ARE NOT ALLOWED TO SMOKE. FOOD AND DRINK ARE
SERVED AT THE INTERVALS, BEFORE AND AFTER THE SHOW

"How does this help us to burgle a house?" Smiff asked.

"You'll see," Dreep said. "There is one act there who will help. We will go along and see him after we have made our first call. A call on our friends, the police!"

Alice had swallowed her second scone and washed it down with steaming tea. She almost choked on it now. "Police? Aren't they the new law in town?"

"They are, Alice. Two finer men you couldn't wish to see . . . in a zoo. Smiff and I met them this morning." He looked up at the clock on the kitchen wall. "Six o'clock? They will be in the new police station now, writing up their reports of last night's duty. They won't set out to patrol the town till after eight tonight."

"You mean we have to do our burglary and be back here before eight?"

"No. We can't do that because the rich folk won't leave their houses till almost eight," Dreep explained.

"So . . . if we can't burgle before eight and

we can't burgle after eight then when do we get to do the job?"

"After eight."

"But the new police blokes will be out. They could catch us with bags full of stolen swag."

"But you have already thought of that, remember?" Dreep asked. "Send them off to some other part of town while you burgle a mile away, you said."

"So I did," Alice nodded. "Cracking idea, though I say it myself."

"You will go to the police station and you will tell them about the burglary that will take place tonight."

"We don't know where that will be yet, do we?"

"We know it will be somewhere on the South Hill side of town."

"So we send them anywhere but there?"

"It's what the gentlemen who go shooting call a 'decoy'. You will tell them there is to be a burglary far away from the place we plan to burgle. They will go to watch the decoy place.

We will know they are safely out of the way."

Alice nodded. Then she frowned. "Why can't Smiff do it?"

Dreep nodded. "You, Alice, are a good little actress. You put on a wonderful act when you pretended to spill your matches in the street. And, of course, the police constables saw Smiff with me this morning. They are not the brightest buttons in the boot box but they may just remember him. You will wear a cap – pretend to be a boy. Then, if things do go wrong. . ."

"Wrong?"

"They won't – but if they do we just stick you in a dress and the boy who gave them the decoy dummy has vanished!"

"All right," Alice agreed. "What do I do?"

And Samuel Dreep told her.

Half an hour later she walked into the building next door.

"Evenin' all!" Liddle and Larch said, looking over the counter at the soot-stained face of a "boy" in a flat cap.

"Evenin' all," Alice said. "Can I speak to

the officer in charge, please?"

Liddle pulled himself up to his full but skinny height. "That would be Inspector Beadle . . . but he never sees anyone. Maybe Constable Larch and me can be of assistance?"

Alice sucked air sharply between her teeth. "Ooooh! I don't know! I have information so-o important, so-o-o-o secret I could be chopped into a thousand tiny pieces for telling you. We are dealing with very dangerous criminals here!"

"Ah," Liddle nodded. "In that case Constable Larch will deal with it. He's not afraid of dangerous criminals, are you Larch?"

"Yes."

Alice shook her head, "Well . . . dangerous for children."

"Children?"

"About my age."

"Oh!" Liddle laughed. "We aren't afraid of kids. What are they up to? Throwing stones at the railway engine? Pinching socks off washing lines?" he chuckled.

"Or worse!" Larch laughed. "Knocking

on doors and running away!" The two men roared with laughter.[23]

"Burglary," Alice said.

The men stopped laughing.

"Oh, that is serious!" Larch agreed.

"They could hang for it," Liddle nodded. "At the very least they could be sent off to Australia for fourteen years."

"At the very least. Cruel place, Australia. It's on the other side of the world where people walk upside down."

"The blood would rush to your head!" Liddle cried. "Terrible. You'd be better off getting hanged in the comfort of your own town."

"Not that being hanged is what you'd call comforta—"

"STOP!" Alice screamed. "Stop!"

The two men looked at her as if they had forgotten she was there. "Evenin' all?" they said.

---

23 Foolish men. They don't know what you and I know. If a kid nicks your pocket watch then the watch stays as nicked as if my granny had taken it. In fact there were so many thieving kids around in the 1870s they invented schools to get them off the streets! Never scoff at a thieving child or you'll lose your watch. . . if you don't watch it. Master Crook knew that.

"At nine o'clock tonight two burglars will break into the Wildpool hospital."

"Why? Are they sick?" Liddle asked.

"They wish to steal bottles of laudanum," Alice said quietly. "Posh people have nannies to bring up their children," she went on.

"I was brought up by a billy goat cos my parents couldn't afford a nanny!" Larch laughed. Alice glared. Larch said, "Sorry. Laudanum."

"Nannies give laudanum to babies to send them to sleep and shut them up so they can have a quiet life," she said.

"Or gin! That's good for babies," Larch said. [24]

Alice said, "Nannies pay a sovereign for a bottle of laudanum. Catch the burglars at the hospital and make Inspector Beadle proud of you."

"And Mayor Twistle!" Larch said. "We could even get a medal. We'll be there. Outside the hospital. . ."

"Hiding in the bushes," Alice said. "Between eight o'clock and ten o'clock."

24 If you have a squalling baby brother or sister in your house please do NOT give it a spoonful of gin. The kindest way to deal with squalling babies is to take a large roll of cotton wool. Stick it in your ears. Problem solved. Don't thank me. It 's all part of Mr X's service.

"Eight and ten. We'll be there," Larch promised.

"Good," Alice said with a rare smile.

"Now, young man, there could be a reward if this leads to an arrest. Give us your name and address," Liddle said and picked up a pencil.

"No reward," Alice said in the voice of an angel. "I am proud just to serve my town and do my duty to Mayor Twistle."

The girl turned on her heel and ran from the station. Two constables looked after her. "What a noble young man," Liddle sighed. "Noblest of the noble. It gives us hope for the future of our world. If only all young people were as . . . as. . ."

"Noble?"

"Noble."

"Reminded me of someone," Liddle said, sucking on the end of his drooping white moustache.

"Reminded ME of the little match girl we nicked pennies from," Larch muttered. "But he couldn't be."

"Impossible," Liddle agreed.

"Anyway, the lad's information means we'll have two arrests tonight. Inspector Beadle will be pleased!" Larch chortled.

"Who's the other one?" Liddle asked.

Larch pulled out the piece of paper from the back of the report book. "Orders from Inspector Beadle."

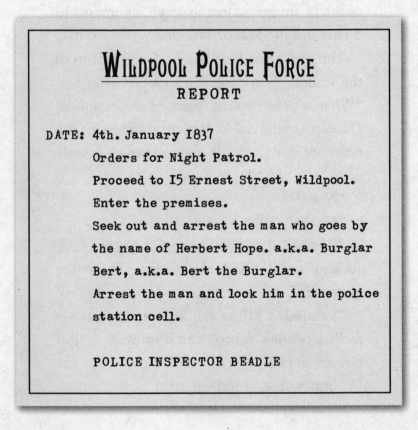

WILDPOOL POLICE FORCE
REPORT

DATE: 4th. January 1837

Orders for Night Patrol.

Proceed to 15 Ernest Street, Wildpool.

Enter the premises.

Seek out and arrest the man who goes by the name of Herbert Hope. a.k.a. Burglar Bert, a.k.a. Bert the Burglar.

Arrest the man and lock him in the police station cell.

POLICE INSPECTOR BEADLE

"Right, Larch, we've a busy night ahead of us. Better be off!"

Smiff Smith also had a busy night ahead of him. The snow was still more like frozen rain than the big fluffy flakes you see on Christmas cards. It blew across the cobbles and rattled against the ice puddles.

Smiff was happy in his new boots. Samuel Dreep led the way to the Apollo music hall, turned into a back lane from the side and went in through the stage door.

The doorkeeper looked up from his desk. "Can I help?" he asked and stroked his thick sideburns as if he were important.

"We have come to see your star. The Spirit Master," Dreep said as he brushed snow off his shoulders on to the doorkeeper's well-swept floor.

The man scowled but said, "Down the corridor. Third door on the right. The door with the star on it."

Dreep swept his hat off and gave a bow. Snow from the hat scattered on the floor. He marched along the corridor. Smiff's nose picked up a rich mix of smells – sweet perfume from the dancing girls, greasepaint and powder from the actors and ale and cigar smoke from where the audience would be sitting.

"Where's the elephant?" he asked. "I can't smell elephant?"

"It's a trick. It's a girl in an elephant's costume," Dreep explained then knocked on the door with a silver star on it.

"Come!" came a booming voice from inside.

The visitors stepped inside. The Spirit Master stood there. A handsome man with blazing brown eyes and long dark hair swept back from his forehead. "Good evening. . ." Dreep began.

The Spirit master raised a hand. Dreep fell silent. The showman looked at Smiff. "Careful, boy, I can read your mind!"

"I hope not!" Smiff squawked.

"You have a curious name . . . I see a name beginning with 'S' . . . stiff . . . skiff . . . Smiff!"

"Amazing!" Smiff gasped.

"I see a steep row of houses . . . poor houses. And a woman . . . a woman with a cupboard full of mop buckets . . . this woman . . . is your mother. . ."

"Yes, my mother IS a woman!" the boy cried in wonder.

"And you have just changed jobs . . . you were a shop-thief but now you are going for greater things . . . burgling fine houses, I think."

"That is incredible!" Smiff choked. "If you can read everyone's mind like that . . . why . . . there would be no crime! You'd just tell the police what all the villains are thinking. We're done for, Mr Dreep! Done for!"

Dreep threw back his head and laughed. He looked at the Spirit Master and said, "Knock it off, George. Save the mind-reading for the audience."

"But Mr Dreep . . . he CAN read minds. He knows all about me!" Smiff insisted.

Dreep shook his head. "He can not read minds. He knows all about you because I told him all about you last night after I met you. It's all a trick."

"It fooled me," Smiff said angrily.[25]

_____

25 Well, you can't blame Smiff. You would be angry if someone made you look stupid. Or you might be angry. I mean some people look stupid from the day they are born! Look in a mirror and you might spot one of those people! Hah! Only joking.

George, the Spirit Master, didn't look too happy either. "Oh, Samuel, you have to spoil things, don't you?"

"Sorry, George." He turned to the boy. "The truth is George does have a wonderful act. He guesses things about people and amazes them. He also has the most wonderful memory. He sees someone once and he remembers everything about them. He can answer every question that the audience call out to him. And that's how he can help us!"

Smiff was interested now. "How can he help us?"

Dreep explained. "Many of the rich folk of Wildpool will come along to see the show. George will look out into the audience and he will recognize a lot of the faces. If those people are here tonight then they are not at home!"

"Those are the homes we can burgle! I get it!" Smiff cried. "Oh, but how does Spirit Master tell us? I mean he can't say . . . 'I see we have Mr and Mrs Jones here tonight from 71 Frith Road. Pop off and burgle their house, Smiff.' I mean he can't!"

"No," Dreep agreed. "He will use a secret code. Tell us, George."

And George the Spirit Master told the boy exactly how the code would work.

Chapter 5

LIGHT OF LIME

Liddle and Larch stepped into the cold street. They clattered along with truncheons and handcuffs, lanterns and rattles all swinging from their belts. A deaf thief would hear them coming two miles away.

They marched, in step, past the darkened house next to the police station . . . a house with a red door and a sign that read, "Master Crook's Crime Academy".

"Did you lock the door behind us?" Larch asked.

"Nah! I think Inspector Beadle is still in the building."

Larch nodded. "We don't see much of him, do we? Since he gave us the jobs, I mean."

"He spends a lot of time in his office. He is plotting to overthrow the criminal musty minds of Wildpool."

"I think you will find that is 'master' minds," Larch said. "Anyway he was in there when we went home to bed this morning."

"Was he?"

"I could hear his clock ticking in the office."

"Ah!"

"And he was there when we signed on duty tonight!" Larch said.

"Clock ticking again?"

"That's right." Larch stopped and shook snow off his boots. "Here! Maybe he never went home. Maybe he sleeps in the station."

"Caw!" Liddle cawed. "What a man."

"No! No! No-o!" Larch said. "Remember who it is who goes out into the night, arrests burglars, hides in bushes, nabs thieves. Who's that?"

"Dunno."

"You and me, Liddle. You and ME!"

"True. But we haven't arrested anybody. Not yet."

"Aha! But we are just about to," Larch told him.

"Ah," Liddle nodded. His cheeks were being whipped by his wispy white moustache waving in the wind. He stepped on the legs of a blind beggar who lay in the shelter of a shop doorway.

"Here!" the beggar called. "Watch where you're walking!"

"Watch where you're lying!" Liddle shouted back.

"How can I watch anything when I'm blind?"

"Suppose you have a point," Liddle nodded. "Sorry. Evenin' all."

"Good evening Constable," the beggar said with a sad smile.

The constables reached the end of Ernest Street. Just like Low Street, a few roads along, it sloped down steeply to the river. Women in shawls and wooden clogs slithered up to the shops at the top. Larch and Liddle's big boots, with steel studs, skidded and sparked as they stepped carefully down. Liddle counted,

"One . . . two . . ." until he reached ". . . fifteen. Here we are, Larch. The house of Bert the Burglar."

"Are you sure?" Larch asked.

"There's no number on the door," Liddle said.

"Ooooh! We don't want to go barging in, hitting people with our truncheons, handcuffing them up and dragging them back to the station if they're the wrong people, do we?"

"I see the problem," Liddle said. "Tell you what . . . if there is a bloke inside we'll come right out and ask him. 'Are you Bert the Burglar?' we'll ask him."

"Clever, Liddle. Very clever. I can see why you got the job," Larch chuckled.

"Let's hope this is the right number," Liddle muttered. "We haven't got all night to search all the houses. We have to get across the river to the hospital," Liddle said. "I mean I THINK I counted right.[26]

---

26 The truth is he had run out of fingers to count on when he reached ten. I would be the same, I don't know about you. Anyway, he tried to use his toes but they were froze together. If you have two toes froze together, do they count as one? I don't knows.

People should get numbers put on their doors, you know. Instead of these stupid little signs."

"Sign?" Larch asked. "What sign? What does it say?"

Liddle's dark lantern had a narrow slot in the front to let out the light but keep out the wind. He shone it on the sign.

HERBERT HOPE

a.k.a. Burglar Bert.
a.k.a. Bert the Burglar.
Apply within for all your
burglarizing needs
No job too small, no lock too tough
Also windows washed, gardens
weeded and odd jobs done

"What's 'a.k.a.'?" he asked.

"Also known as," Larch explained.

"Nah! That would be 'a.n.a.'," Liddle argued. "Still this looks like the place."

"I wouldn't trust that sign," Larch scoffed. "If he's a burglar he could be lying! He might really live next door! That's what I would do if I were a burglar."

"Let's give it a shot," Liddle said and rapped on the door with his truncheon.

"What did you do that for?" Larch asked.

"I didn't want to hurt me knuckles," Liddle told him.

"No! I mean why are we knocking? We're the police on the trail of a criminal. We should just march in. Catch him by surprise."

"Right then," Liddle said.

"Oh, it's too late NOW," Larch groaned.

"Who's there?" a voice asked from behind the door.

"Police. Open in the name of the law!" Larch roared.

The door opened. "Evening!" Bert said brightly.

"Bert the Burglar?"

"That's me."

"We arrest you in the name of the law," Larch said. He turned to Liddle. "Get out your notebook. . . Now Burglar Bert, a.k.a. Bert the Burglar, anything you say may be written down and used in court."

"Knickers!" Bert said.

"Pardon?"

"Knickers. Go on – take it down. I don't care," the old thief said happily.

"But we are going to lock you up for the night. You will appear in court in the morning."

Bert grinned, "Hang on while I get me coat. Looks chilly out there." He put on a heavy brown coat and pulled on a large cap. "Right, lads. Off we go!"

He stepped on to Ernest Street, closed the door behind him and said, "Right, lads. Let's be off!"

The policemen struggled to keep up with the burglar as he walked up the street to the top and turned towards the police station. "You seem almost happy to be arrested," Larch panted.

"I don't mind, son," Bert shrugged. "I have never done a crime in Wildpool so you'll have to let me go . . . but while I am in your police cell I can't be out burgling places. If somewhere gets burgled tonight then you can't blame me. So, come on, let's get to that cell and I hope you have a nice coal fire on there and a cup of tea."

Larch jogged to keep up with Bert. "What burglary?" he asked. "You mean the hospital job?"

"Ah!" Bert cried happily. "You heard about that then? It's the talk of the town, isn't it? The sooner you lock me up the sooner you can get off to catch them in the act."

Bert began to whistle as he marched past Master Crook's Crime Academy and straight through the front door of the police station. He walked into the cell, slammed the door shut behind him then took out a piece of wire. By the time Liddle and Larch had caught up, the old man had used the wire to make a skeleton key and lock the door. "It's all right, lads, I'll light the fire myself. I'll be snug and warm while you two go and freeze in the hospital hedge. Have a nice night!"

Liddle and Larch looked at one another. They were quite pleased to have made their first arrest. But there was something wrong about it. Something neither man could put his finger on.

"Do you think," Larch said, "we should tell Inspector Beadle we have a suspect in the cells?"

Liddle nodded. "Good idea. I mean . . . he'll be in charge of the building while we are out with our truncheons of crime, fighting fires."

"Truncheons of fire, fighting crime, you mean," Larch said.

They stood at the top of the stairs leading down to the basement. "His clock's ticking," Liddle said.

"You go down first," Larch said.

Liddle stuck out his chin and walked carefully down the wooden staircase. He tapped on the navy blue door at the bottom.

"Enter!" said the deep but soft voice.

The large shape of the inspector was planted on a chair. Wobbling bits of fatness seemed to spill over. The inspector's sharp eyes made the constables nervous. The clock tick sounded like a horse's hoof on an iron roof.[27]

---

27 And the clock tock sounded just as loud. Of course you don't often hear horses' hooves on iron roofs – maybe you have NEVER heard them. In that case I will have to ask you to imagine it. For I have only heard it once. "Clip-clop, clip-clop, slip-drop, neigh-splatt." You do NOT want to know what happened.

Liddle spoke quickly. "We have arrested the suspect Burglar Bert a.k.a. Bert the Burglar and have locked him in the cells above, and all he'll say is 'knickers' and we are now on our way to the hospital to catch a burglar who is planning to steal bottles of laudanum that babies give to nannies so they can have a quiet life and we'll arrest them and bring them back and put them in the other cell."

Inspector Beadle nodded slowly, making his chins wobble. He pushed a piece of paper over the desk. "Here is a map of the hospital," he said softly. "You will need it. I have marked the laudanum store with an 'x' and the hedge where you can hide with a 'p'," he said.

"A 'p'?"

"It's a privet hedge."

Constable Liddle picked up the map and slipped it inside his notebook. "Fear not, sir, we will arrest them with our flaming truncheons." He raised his truncheon high above his head.

"Good man," the inspector said softly. "I can see I was right to give you this job. Now go and do it."

Liddle gave a sharp salute and cried, "Yes, sir, ouch!"[28]

The officers rattled up the stairs and out into the night once more. They headed for the bridge over the river and the north bank.[29]

The front doors were open now and people were starting to enter from the street. Alice had joined Smiff and they sat in the back row of the theatre seats with Samuel Dreep.

Gentlemen were taking their seats and lighting cigars. They carried glasses of ale from the theatre bar rooms at the back and chatted while they waited for the show to start.

Ladies in their best bonnets and warmest shawls took their seats. They sipped at little glasses of sherry and gossiped behind the fans they carried.

28 He cried "ouch" because he had forgotten he was holding a truncheon in his saluting hand. Don't feel too sorry for him. His helmet saved him cracking his skull.

29 Of course YOU know that the burglary will take place on the south side of the river. But you only know that because I told you. So don't be too pleased with your cleverness.
After all, you have not worked out how the Spirit Master will get the message to Alice and Smiff, have you? To find that out we need to return to the music hall. . .

As usual Alice found something to be angry about. "Four pence tickets at the back of the theatre. We will see nothing from here. What sort of seats do you call these, Mr Dreep? I can hardly even see the stage for the smoke. If I was the mayor I would ban smoking in places like this!"

Dreep spoke quietly. "Alice, you are not dressed as a rich young lady. You are dressed as an urchin boy. If you sat in the good seats at the front you would be in the middle of all the fine ladies in their ribbons and bows, satin gowns and lace bonnets. People would notice you. The best burglars are the ones who do not get themselves noticed."

Alice pouted. "Who says? You says?"

"And of course, once George, the Spirit Master, gives you the secret message you need to slip out of the theatre without being seen. If you are at the back you can do that easily."

Alice pouted some more. Smiff was too dazzled by the beauty of the theatre to notice his partner's mood. "How do they make that light?" he breathed. Brilliant beams of blue and green swept across the stage as the stage managers practised.

"It's a new invention," Dreep said. "It's called lime-light. It's a gas light but not the same sort of gas they use in street lights. Wildpool is the first theatre in the country to have it outside the capital. It is so special they say the mayor himself will honour us with a visit this evening."

The theatre orchestra were starting to fill the "pit" in front of the stage and blow tunelessly into their instruments, or scrape at their violins to warm them up. Footlights at the front of the stage were lit and their red, yellow, green and blue shades threw a rainbow of light on to the dark stage curtains.

The chatter and laughter changed suddenly. It became an excited babble and the smoking men and gossiping women turned to look up to the rooms at the side that looked down on the stage and were very close to the stage. Little rooms called "boxes" that cost a whole shilling per seat to buy. Only the very rich went in there.

Alice, Smiff and Dreep followed the glances. They saw a large, white-faced, pink-cheeked, scarlet-lipped woman in a green gown like a ship's sail and a bonnet like a spread peacock's tail. She looked down on the smoky masses below and raised a hand in a white silk glove. Just one wave. Then she sat down on her gold-framed seat with satin cushions.

Now the crowd could see the little man with the neat beard who had been standing behind her. He was in a fine black suit with a bow tie and white gloves too. He waved and waved and smiled at the people below.

"Mayor Twistle," Dreep explained. "Always likes to be seen out and about."

"Why?" Smiff asked.

"He wants the people of Wildpool to like him."

"And do they?"

Dreep snorted. "Twistle made his fortune from factories and lands. He used his money to buy the votes that made him mayor. But he will never, ever give money to the people who need it . . . the poor. In Twistle's world the poor would starve to death and leave the town for fine folk like him and his wife Arabella. No one likes Oswald Twistle."

"Except his wife," Smiff argued.

Dreep's great green eyes glittered in the limelight. "Especially not his wife!" he laughed. "In fact I would not be surprised if Master Crook didn't have a plan to fix Sir Oswald."

"Fix? How?"

"I don't know. You never know with Master Crook."

Alice scowled, which made a change from the pout but not much of a change. "Will we get to meet this Master Crook?" she demanded. "I want to see him."

Dreep became serious. "You would NOT want to see him, Alice White. He is more terrible than the nastiest nightmare you have ever dreamed. But you WILL see him if you do something very wrong and upset him."

"You're scaring me," Smiff said.

"You don't scare ME!" Alice hissed. "In fact I don't even think Master Creepy Crook exists.

I think YOU are Master Crook!" she went on.

Dreep turned his gooseberry eyes towards the stage where the orchestra had started playing a jolly tune. "Oh, is that what you think, Alice White?"

"Am I right?" she cried.

"Shush," said someone in front of her. "The show is about to start."

Alice shushed her mouth, but her mind was screaming with questions and anger.

Smiff sat next to her and felt the danger.

Chapter 6

MESSAGE OF MYSTERY

The orchestra played and the curtain rose. Limelight glittered on the bright faces of a group of singers who grinned at the audience as they sang from a sheet that was hung above the stage.

"It's so good to see you here,
We will bring you such good cheer;
We will bring you smiles and tears,
Tasty pies, refreshing beers!"

The audience sang along and laughed. Everyone was in a good mood and for a while even Alice forgot why they were really there. She sniffed away a tear when Mr Edward Edwards came on stage to sing, "If mother could see me now".[30]

"What's wrong?" Smiff asked her.

"I've got a cold in my nose," she lied.

"The song upset you? If your mother could see you now she'd be proud of you," he said gently.

"Who says? You says? Yeah, well she's a bit too dead to see me, isn't she, dummy."

"Sorry."

"Forget it."

When the Highland dancers came on stage she did forget her misery as they whirled to the skirl of the bagpipes. A twirl of tartan to the stamping and clapping of the audience. They left the stage to roars and cheers.

Then the lights dimmed and the compere stood in a small pool of limelight. "And now,

---

30 The truth is she wiped her nose on her sleeve. This is not a pleasant habit but if you can't afford a handkerchief what else can you do? Drip on to your lap? Snot a nice thought is it?

ladies and gentlemen, the most awesome and amazing Apollo act you will ever see, even if you live to be two hundred years old!"

"Oooo!" the audience gasped.

"We proudly present a man with the power to step inside your mind, to read your every thought!"

"Oooo!"

The compere pointed suddenly at a lady in the third row. "So you'd better be careful what you think, young lady!"

"Ha! Ha! Ha!"

"Yes, this man speaks to the spirits of our dear dead friends."

"Oooo!"

"This is not some cheap stage magic trick . . . this is a mindboggling mystery of the universe, brought to you by the fabulously phenomenal, the terrifyingly talented, the confoundingly clever . . . Spirit Master!"

"Hooray!"

The curtains opened. Samuel Dreep's friend George stood in front of plain black painted boards. He wore pale make-up with heavy shadows around his eyes and thin red lips. He said nothing for a few moments. The people in the audience all seemed to be holding their breath.

At last he spoke in a deep voice. "The spirits are with us tonight. There is someone in the audience . . . someone called Jenny!"

"That's me!" about ten women gasped.

"Your dead mother sends greetings across the universe. She is watching over you," the Spirit Master boomed.

"Ooooo!"

Smiff nodded. It was an easy trick . . . pick a common name and you could be sure half of the people with that name would have a dead parent.

But the next trick baffled Smiff. "I want three people to help me!" He pointed to the woman in the second row, "You, young lady?"

She giggled and nodded. He passed a piece of paper, an envelope and a pencil to her.

"Someone from the back, perhaps?"

Samuel Dreep stood up and called, "Me, Spirit Master!" He walked to the stage to collect the paper and pencil. Finally George turned his shadowy eyes on the box by the stage. He handed a sheet to Lady Twistle. She smiled and took it. The Spirit Master said, "I want you to write down three words. Three words that mean something to you. Three words that I could not possibly guess. . ."

They each did as he told them, folded the papers and placed them in the envelopes. They handed them to him. The Spirit Master took an envelope. He held it to his forehead so it hid his eyes. The audience fell silent.

The Spirit Master spoke slowly. "These are the words of the young man from the back. . ."

The audience turned and looked at Dreep, then turned their eyes back to the stage. "The first word is . . . Crook . . . the second word is Academy . . . and the third word is . . . ah, this is so hard . . . I think you have spelled it wrong!"

The audience laughed.

"But the word seems to be S-m-i-f-f . . . Smiff?"

Dreep turned to the audience, "Amazing!"

George opened the envelope, took out the paper and said, "Crook, Academy and . . . Smiff!"

The audience cheered then fell silent again. "The young lady's words are . . . Barney? A boyfriend perhaps?"

The audience laughed and the young lady blushed.

"The second word is . . . handbag? Maybe something you love more than Barney?"

Laughter.

"And the third word is something you love most of all . . . shoes! Am I right?" He opened the envelope and nodded as the girl cried, "I don't believe it!"

Finally he turned to the mayor's wife. "And you, my lady. . ." he pressed the envelope to his forehead and held it there longer than ever. "Ah! My lady, you are really testing me, aren't you? Trying to catch me out!"

Arabella Twistle raised her fan to hide her smirk. The Spirit Master's face twisted in pain as if he were trying to tear the words from the air. "The first word is . . . doodle . . . the second word is . . . humpty . . . and the third word is . . . is simply the letter X. Am I right?" He pulled the paper from the envelope and smiled as

Lady Twistle gasped, "Amazing!"

George passed the papers to Dreep. "Can you check them? I haven't lied?"

"No . . . they are all correct . . . every word!" Dreep said, waving the papers excitedly at the audience.

They cheered as Dreep slipped the papers into his pocket and went back to his seat.

Dreep returned to his seat beside Smiff and Alice. "Can he really read minds?" Smiff asked quietly as George went on with the act.

Dreep explained, "No."

"So how does he do it?"

"He has a friend in the audience. The first words he gave out were mine."

"How did he know what you'd written?" Smiff hissed.

Alice answered. "They decided that before the show. Mr Dreep wrote what they agreed. Easy. Would only fool a dummy."

"But the girl? How did he know her words?"

Samuel Dreep shrugged. "He tore open the first envelope to read my words."

"Yes, I saw that."

"And THIS is what he read," Dreep said, passing the paper to Smiff. Smiff looked at the paper.

**BARNEY
HANDBAG
SHOES**

Smiff frowned. Dreep explained. "George really tore open the girl's envelope, read her words then pretended they were in my sealed envelope."

"I get it!" Smiff cried. "He gave the girl her words – said he was opening her envelope to check, but opened Lady Twistle's envelope and read it."

**DOODLE
HUMPTY
X**

"Correct."

"He gave Lady Twistle the words then opened the last envelope, but that was really your envelope," Alice finished.

The boy looked at the third sheet.

CRIME
ACADEMY
SMIFF

"He's a cheat and a crook," she said.

"Just like us," Smiff laughed.[31]

"Hush!" Dreep said. "This is the part of the show where he gives us our message."

The Spirit Master was giving curious messages to people in the audience. Messages from their dead friends and loved ones. Messages that were such a jumble the people had to make their own meanings.

31 And just like YOU. For, now you know how it works you can try this trick yourself. If you are really good then people will think you are in contact with the afterlife. If you are really bad they will probably throw rotten eggs and squidgy tomatoes at you. But a life of tricks is a life of risks . . . as Alice and Smiff were about to find out.

"A graveyard cat is sobbing for its lost mistress, Juliet, and the toast on the table is burned."

"Yes!" a man cried. "I think that's my Uncle Will speaking to me!"

"Now!" the Spirit Master boomed. "I have a message for . . . Alice. A message from a long-lost friend."

"That's us," Samuel Dreep said softly. "Write down exactly what he says."

"Here is the message, Alice!" the man on stage cried and stared up into the lights as if a spirit was speaking to him from there. "The wind is slight tonight little Ellen . . . unlucky for some – so on until time halts. . . Dream richly, I value everything!"

George gave a nod to show he was finished. Dreep slipped from his seat and Smiff and Alice followed him out of the theatre. Smiff wanted to see the rest of the show. It was a world of dreams in there and he felt he was waking to the cruel, cold, real world when he walked outside.

When they reached the warm classroom of

the Crime Academy, Smiff spread his note on a desk and they read the message.

The wind is slight tonight little Ellen...
unlucky for some - so on until time halts...
Dream richly I value everything![32]

The
wind
is
slight
tonight
little
Ellen
... unlucky for some

so
on
until
time
halts...

32 Now I am sure you have worked out exactly what the message said. You can skip this page and give yourself a large bar of chocolate as a reward. But for the one reader in a hundred, the one who is not quite as clever as a goose with no head, here is what Smiff did with it next. He wrote the words in a list:

> Dream
> richly
> I
> value
> everything!

"There we are," Dreep said. "Take the first letters of each word and it spells out the name and address you need to burgle tonight."

"Yes, I know that, I know that," Alice said crossly. "But what's that bit in the middle? Unlucky for some?"

Dreep and Smiff looked at one another and spoke together, "Number thirteen!"

"I knew that," Alice said with a scowl. "I just wondered if you scarecrow-heads had managed it. Well done."

"So-o," the boy nodded. "The victim is Twistle and the address is 13 South Drive. That's up the hill to the south, isn't it?"

"It is. Now Mayor Twistle is at the show. It won't finish till ten o'clock at the earliest and you'll be back here long before then. But, just to be on the safe side, George will send them a message inviting them to have dinner with him in the star dressing room . . . people like the Twistles will love that. They won't get home till eleven o'clock or even midnight. The constables are across the river so all you two need are your burglary kits!"

Smiff and Alice collected the bags of crowbars and skeleton keys, swag bags and dark lanterns. As they were about to leave there came a curious and eerie whistle. "What was that?" Smiff squeaked.[33]

"A whistling wall!" Alice said. "I've never seen one of those before!"

Dreep chuckled. "It is a dumb waiter."

"Who says? You says? Doesn't sound very dumb to me!" Alice grumbled.

"When this building was a house THIS room was the dining room. The kitchens were down in the basement. The food was sent up in a little rope lift set in the wall." Dreep

33 He was getting nervous and that's why his voice squeaked. That's why mice squeak when they are chased by a cat. Nerves. You never hear a mouse shouting "You can't catch me, cat," in a deep voice, do you?

opened a small door in the wall.

"But what's the whistle?" Smiff asked.

"Someone below blows into a tube in the kitchen and there is a whistle in the other end of the tube up here in the dining room."

He took the paper and drew a quick sketch to show how it worked.

"Pull the whistle out at this end," Dreep explained, doing just that. "Put your ear to the tube . . ." which he did. ". . . and when someone speaks into the tube below you can hear it up here! But first give them a whistle to show you're ready."

Dreep placed the tube to his mouth, blew and then spoke into it. "Hello!"

He placed it back to his ear and listened long and hard giving grunts and nods from time to time. Smiff turned to Alice, "There must be someone downstairs!

"Brilliant. Smiff, I'd never have worked it out," she said. "Now, if you're so clever, tell me who it is? Hah!"

"Master Crook!" Smiff shot back.

"I told you, Dreep is Master Crook and. . ."

Before she could finish the man sent a message back down the tube. "Yes, sir, I understand. I'll tell them." He placed the whistle back in the end of the tube and hung it up beside the dumb-waiter door.

"Master Crook has some . . . worrying news. . ."

"YOU are Master Crook," Alice sighed.

Dreep smiled. "So who was I just speaking to?"

"No one," she said quickly. "You just stuck that tube to your ear and pretended to chat to someone. An old trick but you can't fool me."

Dreep just kept smiling. "And how did I run downstairs, blow in the tube till the whistle went, run upstairs to answer it? How did I do all that without leaving the room?"

Alice looked furious. Her mouth moved but no words came for a while. Smiff had to hide a smile behind his hand. At last she said, "Yes, well, there's someone down in the basement. . ."

"Master Crook," Dreep said quietly. "And he has a message. It seems our friend and teacher, Bert the Burglar, has been arrested and locked up in the police station next door."

"Poor Bert!" Smiff cried. "Will he be all right?"

"Oh, yes," Dreep said. "He WILL be . . . because Master Crook says that after you've done the burglary you can break into the police station and set Bert free!"

"Can we?" Alice snapped. "Why should we?"

"Because," Smiff said, "we have to stick together. When it's your turn to get locked up then you know we'll all come and help to get you out. Isn't that right, Mr Dreep?"

"I will NOT get caught!" Alice raged.

"We all think that," Smiff shrugged. "But it could happen."

Of course, as he spoke, he didn't know just how soon his words would come true. It was almost as if he was the Spirit Master looking into the future – the very near future.

Chapter 7

SHOW
SNOW

Constable Liddle and Constable Larch shivered. They hid in the bushes and looked across the snow-covered lawns of the hospital. "Why can't these burglars do their burgling on a nice sunny day?" Liddle grumbled. The snow was sliding inside his hard leather collar and making his neck sore.

Larch muttered, "If Inspector Beadle knows so much about this robbery then why isn't he out here?"

"Because it's snowing and cold and he's sitting back at the police station in front of a blazing fire," Liddle told him. "That boy that looked like the little match-girl that told us about the burglary. I bet he's not shivering like us!"

But Liddle was wrong.

Alice wrapped her thin jacket tight around her thinner body and headed into the snow. The wind had now dropped and the snowflakes were huge and soft . . . just like on Christmas cards.[34]

The map that Samuel Dreep had drawn for her was getting wet. They climbed the hill towards the rich part of town. The front doors of these houses were at the end of sweeping drives for the carriages. Railings kept out stray dogs, fine trees inside the fences gave shelter from the winter snows or shade in the summer sun.

At last they reached South Drive. Alice turned to Smiff and reminded him, "Walk along the front, Bert the Burglar said. Get a feel for the way the house is laid out."

"But enter at the back where no one can walk past and see you," Smiff nodded. Their voices were muffled by the softness of the snow.

---

34 Except on Christmas cards they are painted on cardboard. They don't melt on your face and dribble cold water into your eyes. Christmas card flakes don't cling to your boots and trickle in at the ankles; they don't turn your nose blue. In fact the huge soft flakes were nothing like the ones on Christmas cards. I wish I hadn't said that. Forgive me.

There was no one to see them in that wintry street. But carriage tracks showed that the people of South Drive could come past at any time. They slipped inside the shelter of number thirteen's gateway. The high iron gates were open. They'd be closed after the Twistles came back from the music hall.

They looked up at the silent house. "The front door is in the middle so the stairs will be in the middle. When we get in you check the bedrooms to the right of the landing and I'll do the ones to the left," Alice said. "That's where the jewels will be – in the bedrooms."

Smiff nodded. "The show will be over soon. We'd better hurry. Just in case they don't go to dinner with George the Spirit Master. They may want to get home before the snow gets too deep."

"You aren't as stupid as you look, Smiff," Alice said sourly.

"You are as clever as you look," the boy told her then muttered, "Not very."

"Let's find the back lane," Alice said.

They ran down South Drive to the end,

turned right then right again so they were in a
dark, narrow lane that ran behind the houses.
"How will we know which one is number
thirteen?" Smiff asked. The wall that ran
along the back was broken up with gates to
the carriage houses as well as small doors.
Some houses seemed to have two back doors.
It made counting tricky.

There was no light in the lane but the snow
gave the doors a glow and showed there were
brass numbers nailed to the doors. "So the
delivery men know where to go," Alice said
pointing at one of the numbers.

They found number thirteen around the
middle of the row. The back gate was bolted.
There was broken glass set into the top of the
wall to keep out burglars. But there was a gap
between the top of the wooden door and the
frame. A gap too narrow for burglars like Bert,
but just wide enough for someone as bone-
thin as Alice.

Smiff lifted her up, she grasped the top of
the door and pushed her head through the gap.
Then she wriggled her body through. Her legs

followed and she managed to grab the door frame to stop herself shooting through and landing on her head. She pulled the bolt open. The gate stuck in the drift of snow but with Smiff pushing from the outside he opened it. He kicked away the pile of snow so the gate opened still wider. "What you doing?" Alice snapped. "You're in."

"But when we come out this way we'll have all the loot, won't we?" he explained. "We need it to open wide."

"Oh . . . yes . . . well, I knew that," Alice said and led the way up the back yard path to the rear of the Twistle house.

Half a dozen steps led up to the back door and half a dozen led down to a door in the basement. "Which door?" Smiff asked.

"The higher one if we want to get to the bedrooms."

Smiff trotted up, pulled out his skeleton key and tried to open it. "No use," he said. "There's a key on the inside of the lock."

"We can turn it and push it out. Bert showed us."

"I know, but it will take time. The basement might be easier."

Alice nodded. She led the way down the steps. She turned the handle of the door. She turned to Smiff. "It's open!"

The door led into a small corridor. Alice opened her leather bag and took out her lantern and matches. She lit the candle and closed the lantern front so just a narrow beam of light shone out. A solid oak door stood in front of them. Alice turned the door knob and felt the door move smoothly inwards. "This one's open too!" she said and almost smiled.

"Great!" he grinned. "It's our lucky day!"[35]

Bert the Burglar sat by the fire in the police station cell. He had unpicked the lock, wandered out and found some cheese and bread in the constables' room. He made himself a pot of tea and took it back to his cell to sit there in comfort. As the coal sizzled he shook his head. "I feel bad," he said to the

---

35 Of course, it never works like that, does it? A wise man once said, "If something looks too good to be true then it probably IS." And YOU can see what was wrong, can't you? A rich person would only leave the door to the house open if. . . ?

fire. "I have burgled since I was a boy. I know everything. But I don't always remember what I know, do I? I mean, that's how I came to get caught last time, wasn't it? How did I come to get caught?"

The fire spluttered at him but didn't give a sensible answer. Bert scratched his head. "Let's see . . . I picked a posh house. I made sure the owners were out – just like those kids tonight. I did everything I told them to do. Checked it from the front . . . went round to the back. Climbed over the back gate and went to the back door. Two back doors . . . the upper one leads straight into the dining room, the bottom one leads into the basement."

Bert held the poker in his hand and twisted it in the glowing coals as you would twist a door knob. "That's it! I remember now! The basement door was open. And if I had remembered I'd have known what that meant! A rich person would only leave the door to the house open if . . . oh, dear! Oh, dear. Oh-dear-oh-dear-oh-dear!"

Constable Larch felt as stiff as one of the branches on the bush he was hiding under. Yet suddenly he went stiffer. "Liddle!" he hissed. "Look! Someone coming out of the back door of the hospital."

"The burglar," Liddle said. "He must have sneaked in when you were asleep!"

"I was NOT asleep! I was just . . . just closed my eyes to keep my eyeballs warm."

"Look . . . he's walking across the lawn to that little hut."

Larch pulled out the plan that showed the hospital.

Larch jabbed a finger. "That's us here. . ." he said.

"Ooooh! We look like bushes, don't we?" Liddle said.

"These are bushes," his partner sighed.

"I thought you said they was us?"

"No, no . . . these are the bushes we're hiding under."

Liddle grinned. "If we are under the bushes that explains why you can't see us on the plan!" he nodded happily and snow slipped off his tall hat.

Larch sighed. "That man has come out of the medicine dispensary," he said pointing at the plan. "Looks like he's gone into the toilet!"

"Ah, yes, well even a burglar has to go sometimes," Liddle said.

"So let's catch him!" Larch cried, jumping up. "Oooof! Me knees is stiff! Hurry before he's finished."

"Catch him with his pants down!" Liddle said. "That's not very fair, is it? I mean even a burglar has to have some private moments, doesn't he?"

But Larch wasn't listening. He slithered through the snow to the hut, waving his rattle. In his other hand he carried his truncheon and he used it to hammer on the toilet door. "I arrest you in the name of the law. Come quietly and you won't get hurt. Come out with your hands in the air!"

Liddle arrived just in time to see the door swing open. Light spilled from the hospital windows and lit the face of the man inside. A middle-aged man with thin hair stuck across his scalp to cover the bald patch. His face was a mask of terror. "What's wrong?" he asked.

"I said put up your hands!" Larch shouted fiercely.

The man raised his hands.

His trousers fell down.

"Pick up your trousers . . . and raise your hands."

The man tried to do both. It wasn't easy. "What have I done?"

"Stolen from the hospital."

"No I haven't!"

"Aha!" Liddle said. "We just watched you come out."

"I work there . . . but I needed a widdle. If wanting a widdle's a crime then it's a new one to me. I've never heard of that law before," the man moaned.

"We had a tip-off from a boy . . . who looked a lot like a girl dressed as a boy. A burglar is out to steal laudanum from the hospital," Larch growled.

"Ah, but I work in the dispensary," the man said. "We never use laudanum."

"You don't?"

"Your tip-off must have been wrong," the man moaned.

"Yes," Larch nodded. "We thought that, didn't we, Liddle?"

"No, Larch."

"Well, I thought it. But it is our duty to check out all reports – even the unlikely ones. Now, sir, we'll let you get back to work."

"But. . ."

"Come along, you don't want to hang around here getting cold and we have arrests to make back in the town . . . especially a girl dressed as a boy."

"But. . ."

"Your hospital is safe while Larch and Liddle are on patrol, sir. Back you go."

"But . . . but. . ."

"Run along now!"

"But I haven't had my widdle and I'm bursting!" the man cried.

"Ah . . . yes . . . we'll be getting along, sir. Hope we didn't scare you." Larch said and stretched out a hand to shake the man's hand.

The man shook hands . . . and his trousers fell down.

"Evenin' all!" Liddle and Larch said together as they hurried back across the bridge to the south side of the river. They would be back at the station much earlier than anyone expected, of course.

Mayor Twistle beamed his best smile and Lady Twistle fluttered her fan. "Oh, Spirit Master, we would love to have dinner with you!" her ladyship said. "Maybe you can see into the future?"

"Yes," Mayor Twistle laughed. "Tell us which horse will win the horse race on the Springwell Fields next month? I could make a fortune!"

George the Spirit Master bowed his head gently. "Show me a list of the runners and I will do my best. Now supper is served in my dressing room if you would care to step backstage. . ."

But as the mayor and his wife sailed out of their theatre box, a worried man with a whip whispered into the mayor's ear. "Oh dear!" Mayor Twistle cried and turned to his wife with a pained face. "Ostler here says the snow is getting heavier. If we don't leave now then the horses will never be able to pull the carriage up the hill. We could be stuck half way."

"Gracious me!" Lady Twistle moaned and her fan fluttered like a wasp's wing. "You can't expect me to walk, Oswald!"

"No dear."

"I was so looking forward to talking with the Spirit Master," she sighed. "And to eating," she said, drooling just a little.[36]

"Don't worry, Cook will prepare us a meal as soon as we get home. Sorry, Spirit Master, some other time," the mayor said briskly as a servant helped him into his heavy coat.

George chewed his lip, anxious. Letting Mayor Twistle go home this early was dangerous. "It would be a disaster!" he said aloud.

36 Do you do that? When you are hungry and you think of food, does your mouth go wet enough to flood the floor? Take a tip from me . . . keep your mouth shut. Nobody loves a dribbler . . . unless it's a football player, of course.

"What would?" Lady Twistle gasped. "Can you see into the future? Can you see us having a coach crash in the snow?"

"Stay in the hotel next door!" George said.

Mayor Twistle stamped his foot. "We have no night-clothes with us, we have no servants, no clean shirt and collar for me in the morning. Nonsense to waste money on an hotel when we live just a mile away! Let's go!"

And before the Spirit Master could think of another story to stall them, they were out of the theatre and into the waiting coach. The mayor would be home much earlier than anyone expected.[37]

Smiff opened the door into the basement room of 13 South Drive. Alice stood by his side.

They looked into the room where a fire burned by the kitchen stove and the heat melted the snow on their hats and clothes. Candles flickered in the draught from the door they had just opened.

Smiff's mouth went dry. He looked around

37 Oh, dear. This is not looking very good for our budding burglars, is it?

the room. "Hello!" he said in a voice as weak as the water that dripped from his cap.

"Hello," Alice echoed.[38]

---

38 You don't need me to tell you what had gone wrong, do you. You don't need me to tell you what Bert forgot to tell his jewel-snatching students.

You have already guessed, haven't you?

Chapter 8

GREEN FIRE

Smiff and Alice looked into the surprised faces of the Twistles' cook, the Twistles' butler, the Twistles' footman and the Twistles' maid-servant. "Good evening," the grey-faced, grey-haired butler said. "You must be burglars. Do come in and close the door. There's a terrible draught."

"Oh," Alice and Smiff said together.

"You see," Burglar Bert said to the fire, "there will be TWO back doors. The upper one will lead to the dining room in the house. The posh people can stroll out, after lunch, into the garden on sunny days. But there will be a second door to the basement. That's the one the servants use. They take in the deliveries. It leads to the kitchen. Now," he told an orange and purple flame. "Now . . . if the master and the mistress of the house are out the servants will not be in bed. They will be waiting to serve their master when he returns. They'll wait in the kitchen. So, whatever you do, do NOT go through the basement door."

The old man took the poker and stirred the fire. "That's the mistake I made. Ended up in prison for five years, didn't I?" The fire didn't reply. "I should have told my students that. Never mind, they may use a bit of common sense and work it out for themselves. They m-a-y get away with it." He shook his head. "I hope."

Constable Larch was warm and red-faced as he hurried over the town bridge. His chubby cheeks shone like apples . . . and not green apples. The sounds of the hammers and furnaces in the shipyard below were softened by the snow.

He had scribbled notes into his notebook. They were later printed up in the first Wildpool Police patrol report.[39]

WILDPOOL POLICE FORCE

Constables Larch and Liddle proceeded to
Wildpool Hospital and proceeded to hide under
a bush. There they proceeded to observe
the hospital and apprehended a suspicious
character proceeding on his way to the
little house at the bottom of the garden.
Upon questioning the character he proved his
innocence (he was in the act of proceeding to
empty his bladder) so the officers proceeded
back to the town centre where they suspected a
crime was in the process of proceeding.

39 You will see I have found the report copied on to a Typographer machine. This is so you can read it more easily – and also because Constable Larch's nose dribbled on to the one he wrote in his notebook. It is quite disgusting – go and see it in Wildpool Museum if you don't believe me. Anyway, the speling was rubbish.

The sparking lights and the workers' lanterns glowed bright then vanished behind another squall of snow. Larch was agitated. "You see, Liddle, what this means?"

"No, Larch."

"Someone sent us to the wrong side of town. We, the carriers of the truncheons of fire, are so fearsome they wanted us out of the way. They wanted us at the hospital while they burgled a house somewhere else!"

"Which house, Larch? There are only two thousand in Wildpool. What do you suggest? We search them all . . . a thousand each?"

"Aha! That is why we are policemen, Liddle. We are too clever for the cunning of the common criminal. We can out-think them, can't we?"

"Can we?"

"We can! For a start, if we were sent north of the river the robbery must be taking place to the south. Stands to reason. It will take place tonight . . . maybe at this very moment! And we know it won't be one of the houses by the riverside, will it?"

"Won't it?"

"No-o-o. They have nothing worth pinching, Liddle. No it will be one of the rich houses on the hill at the south end of the town."

"I think you're right – there's just a hundred of them! Fifty each. What do we do? Knock on the door and ask if they've seen any burglars in their bedrooms?" Liddle asked, struggling to keep up with his partner as they marched through the deep snow of the High Street. "Hang on, Larch, I'm not as young as I was."

"You're not as old as the river down there, but it runs a lot faster," Larch grumbled.

There were people pouring out of the theatre, laughing and chatting about the show they had just seen. Some pulled up their collars against the wind and others headed in happy groups towards the tavern.

Mayor Twistle's carriage creaked as it rolled out of the theatre's carriage-yard and on to the snow-covered road.

As the policemen reached the alley at the side of the Apollo music hall they skidded to a stop. A two-horse carriage was rumbling towards the main street and was not going to stop for anyone. The horses' nostrils smoked in the cold air as they strained to pull the carriage through the snow.

Larch held Liddle back so he wouldn't be trampled under hooves or crushed under wheels. "There should be a law against that!" Larch raged.

"Against what? Horses and carriages?"

"No. A law against speeding recklessly. A dangerous-driving law!"

"Hah!" Liddle chuckled. "That'll never happen!"[40]

Suddenly a face appeared at the window. Not a very handsome face. The face was sat on the body of a gnome. "Halt!" the gnome cried to the carriage driver.

The driver pulled on the reins and pulled on the brake. The carriage slithered sideways and came to a halt. Mayor Twistle pushed his head out of the window and waved to the policemen. "You two!"

40 They were wrong, weren't they? In this year of 1901 we now have those motor carriages – a menace on our streets. It was better in the old days when they had a man with a red flag walking in front of the careering cars. Now they can hurtle along at fourteen miles an hour. They say the limit will go up again to twenty miles an hour! What sort of madness is that? Someone will be killed if you ask me.

"Us, sir?"

"Yes . . . come over here and climb on the back of the carriage!"

Larch smiled happily and tugged at Liddle's sleeve to join him. "We'll get a lift all the way to the south hill," he told his partner. He put a foot on the back board of the carriage and hauled himself up. "You want us to sweep the streets of Wildpool clean of the filth that fouls its gutters, your honour?"

"No. I want you handy in case the coach gets stuck in the snow. You two can get off and push," Oswald Twistle snapped. "Home, James, and don't spare the horses!" he cried and slid up the window.

The driver raised his whip. "He loves shouting that . . . even if me name is Jack."

The carriage rolled over snow as white as Lady Arabella's face. It rolled out of the High Street and then the road began to climb the hill towards South Drive and the home of Mayor and Lady Twistle.

The almost-burgled home. . .

Alice was ready for this. She had pictured

the scene in her mind. She threw herself into the act, more dramatic than the Wildpool Pantomime Players, more heart-breaking than Miss Nellie Sherrie (Sentimental vocalist, ballads and opera to bring tears to your eyes).

"Oh, I am undone. Oh, woe, woe, woe! The shame of my crime makes me wring my hands in grief. I know I am a poor and wicked girl. I know they will put the rope around my miserable neck and hang me from the gallows for all the world to see. And with my last breath I will say the words, 'I deserve it!' For I do. But who will pity me, miserable sinner that I am?"

She looked around the table. Four servant mouths hung open. Even Smiff was stunned. Alice's voice rose. "But if . . . if . . . you have one morsel of pity in your hearts then hear my plea! I have walked down life's straight and crooked road and never barked up the wrong tree. Till tonight . . . when hunger drove me to this dreadful crime. Woe, woe. . ."

"Whoa!" the grey-faced butler said, raising a hand. "Stop there, lass. We don't plan to turn you in."

"What?"

"No! We've been waiting years to meet someone like you. Come in, sit down and have a nice cup of tea to warm you up," the cook said. She was a thin thing with hands as red as raw beef from washing and cleaning but her eyes were kind. Alice slid on to a seat beside her and wrapped her hands around a mug of tea. Smiff sat opposite.

"But we came to burgle you," Smiff said.

The footman was a handsome young man with a smooth face and a cheeky grin. "No you didn't."

"Sorry . . . we did!" Smiff argued.

The maid-servant was a lot bigger than Alice – quite a pale-faced pudding of a girl really; her shoulders were broad and strong but bent from carrying heavy trays, turning mattresses, carrying coal buckets, scrubbing floors, washing sheets and heaving heavy shopping up the hill to the house. She spoke softly. "You came to burgle Sir Bossy-Ossie Twistle, not us."

"If we thought we could get away with it we'd burgle him ourselves!" the butler said.

"You would?" Smiff smiled.

"Yes. But we need someone to do the deed and get away. We'd help, of course – show you where they keep all the best stuff. Give you the keys. . ."

"We can pick locks," Alice said.

"Ah, but that takes time. Much quicker if we just open up for you," the cook said.

"Why would you do that?" Smiff asked. "Is this a trick?"

"No trick," the footman said. "But if Nancy were to roll up her sleeves you'd see the bruises where Lady Twistle beat her," he went on, nodding to the maid-servant.

"And I can show you the housekeeping books where if anything is broken the money comes out of our wages," the butler went on. He nodded towards the cook. "Elsie there broke a cup in the washing up. Lady lemon-face Twistle said it was part of a precious set and would cost Elsie a pound in wages."

The cook sighed. "That's a month's wages. And they even make us pay for the food we eat and the tea we drink."

Alice felt the warmth of the fire and the warmth of her temper turning her face red. "So why don't you leave?"

The butler shook his head. "The Twistles would make sure no one else would give us a job. We'd end in the poorhouse. This life is bad but the poorhouse is worse."

"Look. Here is what they ate at their Christmas dinner party they had," the butler said taking a sheet of paper and showing it to the burglar guests.

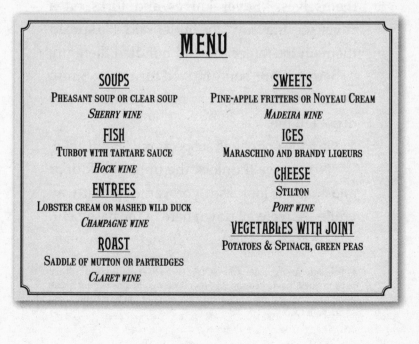

MENU

SOUPS
PHEASANT SOUP OR CLEAR SOUP
SHERRY WINE

FISH
TURBOT WITH TARTARE SAUCE
HOCK WINE

ENTREES
LOBSTER CREAM OR MASHED WILD DUCK
CHAMPAGNE WINE

ROAST
SADDLE OF MUTTON OR PARTRIDGES
CLARET WINE

SWEETS
PINE-APPLE FRITTERS OR NOYEAU CREAM
MADEIRA WINE

ICES
MARASCHINO AND BRANDY LIQEURS

CHEESE
STILTON
PORT WINE

VEGETABLES WITH JOINT
POTATOES & SPINACH, GREEN PEAS

"We get to eat the leftovers," the cook said, "so it's not all bad, is it, Maurice?" she asked the footman. He shook his head.

"So," the footman went on with the story, "we have to get our revenge in any way we can. Some of the things Cook slips into their soup . . . well, you wouldn't want to know."[41]

"But we always hoped one day someone would come along and give them a good burgling. And here you are!" the cook cried.

The servants stood up and busied themselves. "Silver knives and forks on a silver serving tray," the butler said. He spread them on the tablecloth and bundled them up. "There you are, son," he said turning to Smiff. "What's your name . . . no . . . better if you don't tell me."

"But the police will suspect you!" Smiff cried.

"No . . . we'll unlock the upper back door and make it look as if you came in that way while we were all down here in the basement.

41 I am sure, nosey reader, you WOULD want to know. But you will just have to guess. I will just say this. If you ever go to a restaurant to eat, never say anything nasty to the chef. His revenge can be rotten . . . and so can your food.

Don't worry," the butler said. "We've spent many a happy hour talking about this. Planning it. Come on . . . time to head upstairs. There are a few tasty pieces of jewellery that'll make a pretty penny."

"Can't we share them with you?" Smiff asked.

"Better not," the maid-servant Nancy said as she led the way through the dimly lit hall to the stairs. "If we suddenly start to look rich someone will notice."

Maurice the footman shrugged. "We just want to see the looks on their greedy little faces – that will be payment enough for us," he said. And so they started to gather some of the jewels from Lady Twistle's dressing table and slip them into the sack Alice had brought with them.

"Of course Lady Twistle likes to buy a lot of flashy jewellery that's no better than glass," the maid-servant Nancy said. "But I can show you the really valuable pieces – the ones her rich mother left in her will. There are some emeralds that would be fit for Princess

Victoria herself! And please take this solid silver hairbrush . . . it's the one she beats me with."

Nancy opened a drawer and showed Alice the great gems that shone with a green fire of their own. Alice's eyes were wide with wonder. It was almost a pity to hide their beauty in her dusty bag.

"This is so-o easy," Smiff said.[42]

Inside the carriage, the white-faced, pink-cheeked, red-lipped, wig-headed, fan-waving Lady Twistle suddenly called out, "Can't we hurry, Oswald?"

"Why is that, my buttercup?" he asked.

"The Spirit Master has taught me so much tonight . . . I can feel his power in me!" she said and her voice trembled - or it may have been her stomach rumbling with hunger. "I have a bad feeling!"

"A few glasses of champagne will settle you, my dear," he said and patted her knee.

"There is something wrong at the house. I know it, Oswald, I know it. Hurry!"

42 But remember what I said about things that are too good to be true. . .

The mayor sighed but lowered the window. "Home, James and don't spare the horses!"

"I'm going as fast as I can," the driver, Jack, called down from his seat.

"Then it is not fast enough! Get those chaps at the back to push!" Mayor Twistle ordered.

The policemen jumped down and put their backs to the coach. Their boots skidded and they spent as much time falling on their rattles and truncheons and handcuffs as they did pushing. But at last they reached the top of the hill and the end of South Drive.

The horses steamed and snorted like fire-breathing dragons and padded along the drive.

They turned in at the front gates.

If it hadn't been snowing they would have seen that the front door was opening and two small thieves, loaded down with loot, were stepping out.

Chapter 9

SHIP OF SAFETY

Nancy the maid looked down the front drive and was the first to see the carriage lights, glowing in the snowy air. "It's the master!" she cried. "Run!"

"Which way?" Alice shouted into the wind. "No use telling us to run like headless gooses."

"Out the basement door!" the butler said.

Alice was holding the front handle of the solid-silver serving tray and Smiff was holding the back. The loot was piled on top of it. It was clumsy to carry but the burglars had come too far to let go now. They clattered through the house and into the kitchen. They had just reached the basement door as Mayor Twistle reached the front door.

Two frozen, white-coated policeman looked down from the back of the coach.[43]

The mayor had jumped down from the carriage before his driver could open the door for him. He half-dragged his wife from the carriage as she squawked, "Don't be so clumsy, Ossie!"

Mayor Twistle trotted up the steps to where the butler stood by the door. "What's wrong?" he demanded.

The butler twisted his grey hands together in misery. "Oh, Sir Oswald, Sir Oswald, we been robbed!"

"We can't have been!" Lady Arabella Twistle exploded.[44]

"No one would dare to rob the greatest lady in Wildpool!"

"And the greatest man," the mayor chipped in.

"We was all in the kitchen having a little dried bread and dripping for supper," the

43 Yes, I know they had been navy blue-coated, but they looked more like plaster statues, white and solid, after riding a mile as coachmen.

44 I don't mean she actually exploded, of course. That would have left bits of silk dress and fat splattered on the mat. There is nothing so disgusting as a fat-splattered mat. No. Her words exploded.

butler said. "Then Cook thought she heard a sound – a door slam in one of the bedrooms!"

"My jewels!" Lady Twistle screamed and rushed through the hall and up the stairs, fast as a ferret up a drainpipe.

"How did they get in?" Twistle demanded.

"Through the front door while we were in the back?" the butler suggested.

At that moment Constables Larch and Liddle walked stiffly up to the door. "Aha!" Larch said. "There would be footprints in the snow if they had come in this way!"

"Well done, Constable!" the mayor cried.

"Ah!" the butler said and he gulped like a frog swallowing a fat bee. You can see his problem. If the thieves didn't come in through the front door then they must have come through the basement door . . . and the servants must have seen them . . . which they did! It was b-i-g trouble for butler, cook, footman and maid.

But Nancy the moon-faced maid was standing in the shadow of the staircase and heard the policeman. She thought quickly. She pulled the footman towards the dining room at the back of the house. "The dining room door to the garden has to be open!" she said to him. She unlocked the door then threw the key on to the floor. It looked as if burglars had pushed the key out and used a skeleton key.

"Now we need footprints running away from this door, over the snow to the back gate ... then footprints back into the house! Quick!"

The two ran over to the back gate – it was unbolted where Smiff and Alice had just run out.

"Good," Nancy cried. "Now, back into the house!"

They ran back to the dining room door and were in the hallway just in time to bow to the mayor as he and Constable Larch marched through. As Larch said:

WILDPOOL POLICE FORCE
REPORT

Constables Larch and Liddle proceeded through the house to the dining room. The door into the garden was open. Footsteps came into the room and footsteps ran away to

the back gate. This was clearly the means by
which the burglarizing villains had gained
entry. I was about to search the garden for
other clues when Lady Twistle entered the room
and described the loss of her valuables. The
lady was in a very agitated state. She did not
speak polite enough for a police report. But
she said. "The _____ _____ have nicked
me best _____ jewels and the _____ have
left the cheap _____ glass stuff behind.
I want the _____ caught and I want the
_____tortured till they beg to be _____
hanged and I will put the rope round their
miserable _____ necks myself!" Then the
butler pointed out that the solid silver tray
with the silver knives and forks had gone from
the dining room. Mayor Twistle was upset. His
language was even worse than his wife's. He
sort of said, "Oh, dear, they cost a lot of
money. I do hope the criminals will be caught
and punished very harshly."
Mayor Twistle also complained that the
constables were dripping melted snow on to his
expensive carpet and the bill would be sent to
Inspector Beadle.
Constables Larch and Liddle then proceeded to
the front door with Mayor Twistle to report the
theft at the police station.
The constables were asked to ride outside
of the coach so they did not drip on to the
expensive leather seats of the coach.

The coach turned in the drive and rumbled back towards the road at South Drive. It turned slowly. If only the driver had been faster at turning. If only the horses hadn't been so cold and scared of slipping. If only the driver hadn't dropped the whip from his frozen fingers.

If the coach had rolled into South Drive a minute earlier . . . the policemen would have seen two small figures scurrying along, carrying a silver tray between them piled with a bundle of clanking loot. For Alice and Smiff had struggled down the back lane of the houses, through the ever-deeper snow and on to the front of South Drive. There they could trot through the carriage tracks and go much faster. But of course they could be seen by any passing pigeon or postillion.[45]

But the coach was slow. It had to drive around drifts and then it began to slide sideways when it reached the hill down to the

45 Now we have these petrol cars you don't see so many carriages. You young people may not even know what a postillion does! He sits on one of the carriage horses and uses it to guide the others. You could always tell a postillion by his horsey smell. Very smelly things – sweaty horses, but not as smelly as those smoky petrol cars!

High Street. The driver was half-blinded by the snow.

It meant that Alice and Smiff reached the Crime Academy before the coach arrived at the police station next door.

The burglars' faces were glowing as they raced into the classroom and placed the silver tray on the classroom desk.

Samuel Dreep had a warm fire blazing for them and rubbed his twig fingers in glee. "Ah! I can see we have two star academy pupils here. Well done!"

"We were almost caught!" Alice panted. "Barmy old Bert forgot to tell us about the two doors at the back of the house."

Dreep nodded. "Yes, you are so right, Alice. It is time Bert retired. He should go and live with his sister at her little cottage in the country. He's been caught once. If he's caught again it could be the gallows for him. Yes, he's lived a hard life and his last years should be spent in peace."

"Leave burglary to young ones like me and Alice?" Smiff said.

"Exactly!" Dreep chuckled. "That's what Master Crook's Crime Academy is all about."

"So why doesn't Bert just go?" Alice said angrily. "Save us getting caught with his awful advice?"

Dreep shook his head. "Bert's sister is poor as a church mouse, Alice. She can't afford to feed herself let alone her burglar brother. No, Bert needs to take enough cash with him so they can live together in comfort."

"We can give him some of this loot!" Smiff said.

"I hoped you'd say that," Dreep smiled. He untied the bundle and looked at the loot. He divided it into two piles and wrote down what was there.

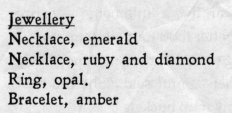

TWISTLE TREASURE

<u>Jewellery</u>
Necklace, emerald
Necklace, ruby and diamond
Ring, opal.
Bracelet, amber

Brooch, turquoise peacock
Pendant, gold and topaz
Ring, silver
Bracelet, silver and jade
String of pearls

72-piece Fiddle, Thread and Shell Cutlery Set.
Dinner knives, sterling silver, 12
Dinner forks, 12
Dessert forks, 12
Dessert knives, 12
Soup spoons, 12
Tea spoons, 12

Extra
Solid silver serving tray – oval, sterling silver,
3 foot wide, ivory handles

"Now, Master Crook has left instructions. He wants half of the winnings to be sold so you two can live a little better – warmer clothes and better food for your families."

"I'm going to buy a brand new mop bucket for my mother!" Smiff said. "She can never have too many mop buckets."

Dreep placed the jewels in his pocket. "I'll take these out of town and sell them for cash." He wrapped the silver knives and forks in the cloth again and tied them. "Now, Master Crook wants you to put these somewhere where the police can find them."

"What! Who says? You says?" Alice cried. "We go to all that risk to steal them and crazy, creepy Crook wants us to give them back? Here . . . let me have a word with him!" She stomped over to the dumb waiter message tube and blew down it. When a low voice answered at the other end she shouted, "Here! What's this about giving our stealings back?" She placed the tube to her ear and listened. "Yeah, but . . . no . . . I see . . . oh . . . we-ell . . . I suppose."

She hung up the speaking tube and turned to Smiff. "There's this new police force in Wildpool," she said.

Smiff just nodded.

"Well, they are not very good . . . and that suits us."

"True!"

"So-o Master Crook says we have to make them look good," Alice went on.

Smiff's eyes went bright. "Great idea! If they fail in this first great crime they'll get the sack . . . Wildpool could get some good policemen and we'd be finished! That's why Master Crook is such a master! He thinks ahead."

"So," Dreep said. "That's agreed." He sat at the desk and looked at the wet burglars. "Now, you have had a tough day's work . . . and I'm sorry, but you're not finished yet."

Alice blew out her cheeks and tried to hold in her anger. "We have to set Bert free, don't we?"

"That was part of your task for tonight," Dreep nodded and spread his fine fingers, helpless. "Sorry."

Smiff shrugged. "I suppose we could give him his solid silver tray, and take the knives and forks to dump where the police will find them?"

"Hang on!" Alice raged. "Bert can't escape in this weather! He can't walk off to see his sister when the roads are choked with snow. It's bad in the town . . . it'll be worse in the country. He'll be dead before morning!"

"Suppose so," Smiff sighed.

"No," Dreep told them, his green eyes twinkling in the firelight. "Bert can head down Low Street to the docks. There's a coal ship leaves on the midnight tide. It'll drop him off down south, he'll get cash for the tray . . . it's all arranged. Set Bert free then get him down to the quayside. Easy."[46]

"The police are up at the Twistle house," Smiff said. "I suppose this is the best time to go and set Bert free?"

"What about Inspector Beadle?" Alice asked.

Dreep smiled. "He'll be snug and warm in his basement, writing reports for the mayor. Don't worry about him!"

Alice and Smiff picked up the tray with the

---

46 Nothing is ever easy in the world of crime, as you have learned. And you, dear reader, can see what is going to happen, can't you? Of course you can! But can you see the way our heroes will get away? Or can you see them swinging on the end of a rope – or worse?

What's worse than swinging on the end of a rope? you ask. Well, being put in a gibbet was worse. You don't see them about these days. But back in 1837 it wasn't enough to execute a criminal. Some of them were taken down after they were dead. Their corpses were painted all over with tar so they didn't rot. Then they were put in a metal cage. The cage was hung up at the roadside so everyone could see them.

There was a famous one at Attercliffe, you may have heard about? It was so very popular and the body didn't rot for forty years!

silverware and carried it back into the snow. The front door to the police station was open and a gas lamp sizzled softly in the entrance hall. A helpful sign said:

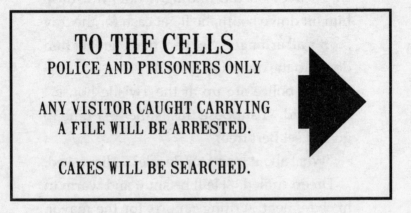

TO THE CELLS
POLICE AND PRISONERS ONLY

ANY VISITOR CAUGHT CARRYING A FILE WILL BE ARRESTED.

CAKES WILL BE SEARCHED.

"Why would they search a cake?" Smiff asked.

"Because, you dummy, friends take a cake to the prisoner and slip a file inside," Alice said.

"In case they fancy doing a bit of woodwork?"

"No – to file through the bars," Alice said growing more angry.

"We haven't brought a file!"

"No, worm-brain, because we can pick locks."

Smiff smiled. "So can Bert."

"True," Alice said shortly.[47]

And when they walked down the passage to the cell they saw the door swinging open. Bert sat inside, poking the small fire. He looked up and frowned. "Oh, there you are! Am I pleased to see you! I was so worried cos I forgot to tell you something in this morning's lesson. . ."

"Too right you did, you old goat!" Alice raged. "You forgot—"

"It all worked out fine in the end," Smiff cut in. "This silver tray is your part of the loot."

The old man smiled happily. "Well done, my star students!" he said.

"Why haven't you escaped?" Alice asked.

Bert frowned. "It's cold out there! I thought I'd stay here snug and warm till the weather turned a bit better," he explained.

---

47 Of course Alice was a short girl. Anything she said would be short. A bit like Mayor Twistle and every one of Snow White's dwarfs. But if you say something "shortly" it means you are a little grumpy. Exactly like ONE of Snow White's dwarfs.

"There's a ship waiting to take you to the port near where your sister lives," Smiff said. "Safer if you leave now. Come on!"

"Safer?" Bert asked. "Why?"

Smiff shook his head. "I don't know why I said that . . . I just have a bad feeling. We shouldn't be in a police station half an hour after we've done a robbery."

"Right!" Bert said. "Let's go before those constables get back."

And so the three burglars slipped quietly into the corridor and walked quickly to the front door of the police station.

They opened it just as a carriage turned into the High Street.

Mayor Twistle opened the carriage door and looked down from the top step. "Bert the Burglar!" he cried. "THAT'S the man that burgled my house! Arrest that man! This time he'll hang for sure!"

"We had him locked away, sir," Liddle said from his step at the back.

"Well he escaped, you buffoon. You can SEE he's escaped. But he won't escape again! Not

with Sir Oswald Twistle on the case. Forward,
James, and don't spare the horses!"

Jack cracked his whip.

Chapter 10

TRAY AWAY

The carriage was dragged past the police station, past Master Crook's Crime Academy at the pace of a greyhound . . . a sleeping greyhound. Smiff's granny could have moved faster and, as you know, she was long dead and on the dung heap. The snow was deep and the whole town seemed silent.

It would have been quicker to walk – the long-legged policemen would have caught the young burglars and their limping old teacher. But Mayor Twistle did not want to wet his fine boots more than he had to.

"On James! Don't spare the horses!"

Jack turned and shouted back, "Maybe if the policemen got out and pushed it would help?"

"Good idea! Liddle! Larch! Off and push!" Twistle roared. "I'll teach Wildpool criminals that it doesn't pay to tangle with a Twistle."

The constables jumped down. The coach moved a little faster . . . but still a lot slower than the policemen if they hadn't had a coach to push. They slithered along, sweat running down under their helmets and stinging their eyes.

The High Street was high above the river.[48]

The workers had given up clanging hammers on the new railway bridge over the river. The workers at the new railway station had come down from the iron roof now. It was too slippery and cold to hold on to the scaffolding.

In the docks the coal was loaded on to the ships waiting for the tide to carry them out into the sea. The gas lights glittered in the streets and Wildpool almost looked pretty in its white blanket.

---

48 Maybe that 's why it was called the High Street. Of course in the heat of summer, when the fly-crusted horse droppings and the sewage-blocked drains made the place stink then some people say it smelled "high". High or high, you decide why.

Alice heard the mayor calling out in the soft, white silence, and shouted, "Hurry, Bert! They'll catch you long before you get down to the quayside."

"If I go any faster me legs'll drop off," Bert groaned. "I'm not as young as you!"

"You're not as young as most of the bones in Wildpool graveyard . . . but you'll be just as dead if you don't hurry up!" she urged.

The old man struggled on till he reached the top of Low Street. The steep street ran down to the river. There was a sharp bend at the bottom end of the road that led to the shipyards. But it was too far for Bert to struggle down the hill.

The carriage was closer now and at last Mayor Twistle saw what was plain as a snowfield. "Stop pushing, you pot-headed policemen! Run after them! You'll easily catch them." He climbed out of the door and worked his way alongside the driver who was panting with tiredness after a mile of whip-waving and rein-slapping.

The police pulled their weary legs through the snow that was now up to their knees and headed towards the burglars at the top of Low Street.

For a moment Alice, Smiff and Bert looked back in horror at the navy-clad nasties coming closer and closer.

"Save yourselves," Bert gasped. "You youngsters . . . don't worry about me. I'll put up a fight. Make sure you get away. Go on! Push off!" he cried like a hero.

The police were twenty paces away now. Mayor Twistle looked on and cheered. "Forward, my brave lads! People of Wildpool! I wish they could see this glorious moment, James."

"We could tell the local paper," Jack suggested.

"No, no! I don't want anyone to know that I was the victim of this crime . . . they may laugh. And anyway, I don't want people to know that I have anything worth stealing! Next thing you know they'll be asking me for money to give to the poor in the poorhouse!"

Fifteen paces away now, Smiff's brain was racing like a greyhound.

Mayor Twistle was jumping up and down with such excitement the coach bounced on its springs. "Men in uniform will patrol the streets and guard our persons, guard our homes, guard our factories and guard our wealth!" he sang happily without his wife's notes to help.

Ten paces . . . then Smiff made his move. "Give me the tray, Alice!" he ordered.

Alice was about to argue but saw the fierce joy in the boy's eyes and let go of her end. Smiff dropped it on to the snow and it sat there shining. He handed the bundle of silver knives and forks to Bert the Burglar. "Drop those off on your way down to the ship!" he said quickly.

"How do I get to the ship?" Bert asked.

"On a sledge," Smiff laughed. "Climb on the tray!"

Bert stepped on to the large silver tray and sat down clutching the silverware. "Ready, Alice?" Smiff asked.

With the policemen just five paces away the young burglars put their hands on the back of the tray and pushed. Slowly it slid down the steep hill of Low Street. When the police were three paces away it picked up speed.

"Whee!" Bert cried in glee. "It's like when I was a kid!"

The snow sprayed away. The policemen stopped to watch the old man vanish downhill, speeding ever faster past lampposts and doors. When he was a small figure at the bottom of the hill he dropped the loot over the side, grasped the front of the tray, leaned to his left and guided the sledging tray round the sharp bend.

"He's escaped!" Mayor Twistle screamed! "Escaped with the loot! I can just see the headlines now . . . oh, how they'll laugh!"

Sure enough the headlines in the paper the next day were not kind to Twistle and his new police force.

5 January 1837

THE WILDPOOL STAR

SNOW HOPE OF CATCHING TWISTLE THIEVES

Thieves raided the home of Wildpool Mayor, Sir Oswald Twistle, during a snowstorm and skated away with some of the Twistle treasure!

Witness Jack Ostler (who does not wish to be named) said, "The old burglar just jumped on a tray and sledged away. The kids that were with him ran off down Low Street and vanished into a house. It was quite funny really!"

Liddle and Larch stopped to watch the speeding man and that gave Alice and Smiff the chance to run and slither down the hill and into Smiff's front door before the constables could catch them.

But Master Crook's cunning plan was not complete, of course. Twistle had seen the cloth dumped at the bottom of the hill and cried, "My valuables! I can get my valuables! Down the hill, James, and don't spare the horses."

Jack turned and said, "Sorry, sir, but we probably couldn't get the coach down that hill without crashing – it's far too steep. And it's stone certain we wouldn't get back up again."

Twistle clenched his hands into fists of fury and beat them against the roof of the carriage. "Liddle!" he shouted. "Go down the hill and fetch my treasure."

"I'll have to dig through those snowdrifts . . . it could be anywhere. Can't we wait till it thaws?"

"Wait? Wait? What if some villains come along and find it first? Do you think they will trot up to South Drive and hand it back to me?"

"They would if they were honest," Liddle argued.

The mayor's eyes were bulging and his face red as a radish as he screamed, "If they were honest they wouldn't be villains, you clown of a constable!"

"That's true, sir."

"As for you, Larch, I want you to arrest Bert the Burglar's accomplices," the mayor went on. "If we can't hang Bert in front of the town jail then we can hang them."

"We don't know if they were there at the scene of the crime," Larch argued.

"It doesn't matter, Constable Clod. I will say I saw them . . . my servants will say they saw them. I want someone hanged."

"Even if they're innocent?"

"Yes . . . even if they're innocent! I will not be laughed at by the people of Wildpool. Now check those houses – find out which one they ran into – arrest them and lock them up . . . and tie them up so they can't unpick your lousy locks."

"Yes, sir," Larch sighed and began to walk

carefully down the steep and snowy street. He followed in the footsteps of Liddle who was half way to the bottom. Larch pulled out his truncheon and used it to knock on doors. The owners of the houses were not pleased.

"Do you know what time it is?" a woman asked.

"Time you had a clock," Larch snapped.

"I was getting my beauty sleep!" she said.

"It wasn't working very well," he said, shining his lantern into her pale face. "I am looking for a couple of boys," he said.

"Try the orphanage," she said.

"Two burglars who ran down here and entered one of these houses. Do you have two boys in the house?"

"No I do not. I have one girl and a very large husband who will not be pleased if I wake him up. Now let me get back to bed. It's freezing."

And so he made his slow way down the hill, one house at a time.

Constable Larch was being watched. He was being watched by Mayor Twistle from the top of the hill and by three people from a door in a house half way down the hill. . .

Mrs Smith peered around the door. "He's five doors away, Smiff. Chubby feller . . . big truncheon. Trouble is you couldn't get enough speed to run past him. One swish of that stick and he'd snap your legs. If you think it's hard running in snow you should try running in snow with two broken legs! Cor! That would be a sight to see."

"Thanks, Mum," Smiff muttered.

"And of course you can't run down the hill cos that other policeman is at the bottom. The one with the droopy white moustache. Oh, yes! Looks impossible!"

Alice stood behind her in the hallway holding a small stump of candle. "Mrs Smith, if that's all you can say then I think I would prefer it if you shut up!"

"Ooooh! Get madam snappy-knickers," she laughed. "I said it looks impossible . . . but the Smith family have been in tighter corners than this and we're still around."

"So, what do you suggest?" Alice asked.

"Mop buckets!" Mrs Smith cackled.

"Mop buckets? Do you have one?"

"One? I've more than one. You can never have too many mop buckets, my dear," the woman said. "Go and get the one from the back kitchen – the one full of cold soapy water – I used it this afternoon to wash the kitchen floor."

Alice scowled but did as she was told. She brought the sloshing bucket to the door. Mrs Smith said, "Good girl. Now watch this!" She opened the door and threw the cold water on to the pavement, just down the hill from her door. Then she closed the door and took the candle into the small living room. The fire had burned out and the ashes were cold now . . . but not as cold as the water on the pavement. That had melted the snow outside and begun to turn into a beautiful sheet of ice.

Two minutes passed. There was a sharp rap at the door from a police truncheon.

Mrs Smith clapped her hands softly and said, "Now, watch this . . . see how a mop bucket can save your life!"

She walked towards the shabby door. Alice and Smiff crept into the hallway and hid behind the door as Mrs Smith pulled it open. "Ooooh! Good evening, constable! I have heard all about you and your partner."

"You have?"

"Well . . . not ALL. I mean, they didn't tell me how handsome you were. I love a man in uniform."

"Yes, well. . ."

"My husband looked smart in his uniform," Mrs Smith said and gave a giggle.

"Was he a policeman?"

"No he was in the prison service," Mrs Smith said, and all the time she kept Larch talking the ice grew harder and the snow was covering the slippery patch.

"Ah, your husband was a prison warder then?"

"No – he was a prisoner at Darlham Gaol. But he did look lovely in that prison uniform. Not as lovely as you though, handsome!"

"Yes, madam . . . now, I am looking for a

couple of boys!"

"Me too!" Mrs Smith screamed in delight.

"What?"

"A couple of nice handsome boys to cuddle me . . . it gets so cold at night, doesn't it? You and your partner are the answer to a maiden's dreams!"

"Madam," Larch said, alarmed, "I am looking for two burglars. They were seen to enter a property on this side of the street. Have you seen them?"

"Oh, those two? Yes! I can show you where they went!" she said and stepped out on to the snowy pavement. "Take two steps down the hill . . . that's right," she went on, guiding him on to the slippery trap she'd laid.

"See? At the bottom of the hill? Searching through the snowdrift?"

"That's Police Constable Liddle!" he said.

"Yes, and you are going to join him!" she laughed. She placed a hand firmly in his back and pushed.

The man's boots scrabbled on the ice patch. They shot forward and into the air. He landed on his plump backside and by then was travelling so fast he ploughed through the snow like a hot knife through dripping.

He stretched out his arms to try to stop himself but it was no use. He sped like a shooting star down the steep hill and then the most amazing thing happened.

He stopped.[49]

---

49 Of course you knew he would. He had to stop some time, didn't he? So what is amazing about that? you sneer. You shouldn't sneer. It makes you look ugly. And, as Smiff's granny used to say, "If the wind changes your face could stay like that." Ugh! Not a pleasant sight.

Chapter 11

CURTAIN OF CROOK

PC Larch stopped with a clatter. A tinkle of silver wrapped in a cloth.

"You found it!" PC Liddle cried. "You found the Twistle treasure! Well done, Larch."

"Ooooh! Me bum!" Larch groaned.

"What's wrong with it?"

"There's something sticking in it."

"Ah, yes, it's a fork. Hang on and I'll pull it out. . ."

"Careful. . . Aaaarrrrgh! Ooooh! That hurt," Larch sobbed.

"Wrap a bandage round it," Liddle shrugged.

Larch struggled to his feet. "The mayor will be pleased," he said.

"The burglar got away," Liddle reminded him. "Sir Oswald was keen to have someone hanged outside the jail. Did you find the boys that were with Bert the Burglar?"

"I think so. I met a very odd woman . . . mad as a three-legged duck . . . but I think she was hiding someone."

"What number house was it?" Liddle asked.

"I forget now . . . I went to half a dozen houses. I guess we'll have to work our way back up the street," Larch sighed.

"It won't be easy getting up the hill . . . not as easy as coming down it."

"Easy? You call a slide that ends with a fork in your bum an 'easy' way to travel?" Larch snapped.

"Sorry," Liddle muttered and picked up the bag of loot. The policemen began to climb the hill but it was slow work. They slipped in the deep snow and clung to the walls of the houses to stay on their feet.

In the Smith house they were just waiting for the police to return, arrest them and hang them. . .

"Well done, Mum," Smiff sighed. "You got rid of the policeman for now, but he'll be back. There are two of them coming up the hill to get us."

"The mayor and his coachman are waiting at the top of the hill if we go that way," Alice put in. "We're trapped."

Mrs Smith shook her head. "Lor! I never met such a gloomy twosome. Remember what Granny used to say."

"Granny said a lot of things," Smiff said angrily. "Then she died and she isn't saying them any more."

Mrs Smith smiled calmly. "Granny always said 'It's not over till it's over'."

"Uh?" Smiff grunted.

But Alice nodded. "Wise words."

"What are you two on about?" Smiff groaned.

Alice's spark was burning again, as bright as the matches she used to sell. "We thought it was all over for Bert . . . but we sent him down the hill on that silver tray and he's free."

"We don't have any more silver trays," Smiff spat.

"No," his mother said cheerfully, "but we have something better. Something that will get you up the hill to the only safe place – Master Crook's Crime Academy."

Smiff frowned. "The police are on their way up the hill. They may be slow but we're slower. . . Our legs are just too short to get through this snow. The mayor and the coachman will stop us if we get to the top."

"Not if you move too quickly to be caught, the way Bert did."

"Bert had a sort of sledge. We can't sledge up a hill!"

Mrs Smith nodded. "There is a place far, far to the north of here. . ."

"Scotland?" Smiff said.

"Even further than Scotland," his mother said. "And it is snow there all the time."

"Impossible," Smiff scoffed. "They couldn't grow food. What do they eat?"

"Fish."

"Is this another one of your stories, Mum?"

"No. This is something your father told me. He didn't always sail on coal ships you know.

Sometimes he sailed up north through seas full of mountains they called icebergs. Look!"

She pointed to a map of the north that was pinned to the wall over the fireplace.

"And that's where he met people who live in snow all the year round. Even their houses are made out of ice bricks.[50]

And he told me how these people get around . . . they wear great plates on their feet. They call them snowshoes. They don't sink into the snow . . . they walk over the top of it. "

"Plates?"

"Try floating an iron nail in a bucket of water and it sinks because it's narrow," his mother explained. "But put an iron plate on the water and it floats because it's so wide."

Alice scowled. "You want us to fasten plates to our feet and go out there?"

Mrs Smith beamed a smile wider than any plate. "I have something better," she said. "Remember what Granny always used to say?"

"It's not over till it's over?"

---

50 Mrs Smith was telling the truth for once. These ice houses, or igloos, are great. Build one yourself and see next winter. Just don't have a house-warming party.

"No, the other thing she used to say – you can never have too many mop buckets."

"Mop buckets?"

"That's right. You put each foot in a mop bucket and grab hold of the handles. They'll work just like snowshoes. You'll walk over the snow. You'll be at the top of the hill before the police can crawl a yard and you can dance round the mayor like butterflies round a lamp post. A short, fat lamp post in Mayor Twistle's case."

"We'll need four mop buckets," Alice said.

"Not a problem . . . I collect them. After all, you can never have too many mop buckets."

Smiff went to the kitchen cupboard and pulled out four buckets. He and Alice slipped them on, grasped the handles and practised walking around the room.

It was clumsy but they soon got the idea.

Outside they could hear sharp raps of truncheons on doors as the constables climbed the hill and came ever closer.

"It's not over till it's over," Alice said. She opened the door and stepped out into the deep snow. Her mop bucket feet hardly sank through the surface of the snow and soon she was speeding up the hill. Smiff was close behind.

"Here! You two boys! Stop in the name of the law!" Constable Liddle shouted. "Stop or I'll call the police!" He waved his rattle. He tried to move but every step was slow and clumsy. He gave up after five painful paces.

Mayor Twistle heard the rattles, and looked down the steep street. "We have them, James! Stop them!"

The mayor jumped down but the snow came above his knees. He was trapped like a wasp in honey.

Smiff and Alice strode past him. "Follow those thieves, James, and don't spare the horses!" the mayor roared but the driver was stuck in the snow as well. By the time they had climbed back on board the burglars had vanished.

Jack, the driver, struggled to turn the coach around. At last it was pointing south again. The two policemen came up to it, panting. "Mayor Twistle, sir, Mayor Twistle!" Liddle cried.

"We have your silverware, sir!"

The mayor's face turned bright as a gas lamp. "See! I knew I could defeat the villains of Wildpool! I knew it!"

And that was the way he told the tale.[51]

Triumph!

Mayor Twistle was delighted with the result, however. "I myself came face to face with the burglars. When they saw me they knew they had met their match. They dropped the loot and ran. They won't be doing any burgling for a long, long time. They know that they just can't get away with it. Not when I am in charge of Wildpool and have the backing of my magnificent police force!"

Mayor Twistle was asked if the burglars got away with anything valuable. He said that they stole a few of his wife's beads and a tin tea tray, but a rich man like him could afford it. One of his forks was bent and had some blood on the end but the mayor did not wish to say how it got there.

Be Aware

House owners of Wildpool are warned to make sure they lock their doors at night and buy a guard dog as a pet. (Guard-cats and guard-goldfish are not so good.)

51 Of course you know that Mayor Twistle stretched the truth a bit. All right, he told a couple of whopping great lies. But Master Crook had been right. Give the victim back half of what you steal and they will think they have won. In fact that's just what Master Crook was about to tell his burglary students. . .

Samuel Dreep was waiting for Alice and Smiff as they clanked through the door of the Crime Academy.

They stepped out of their mop-bucket snowshoes and sank on to seats by the fire. Their clothes steamed in the heat.

Dreep's fingers fluttered in the firelight. "The school will be your home from now on," he said.

Alice shrugged. "I never had a home before so it makes no difference to me."

Dreep nodded. "And you, Smiff? You can't go home to live . . . not in that house now the police know about it."

Smiff sighed. "I can still see my mother, can't I?" Dreep nodded. "Then that's all right. Everyone has to leave home some time, don't they? And the beds here are better than at home anyway!"

That night the student burglars slept deep and dreamless sleeps. They were exhausted by their first day's work. The sun was over the horizon by the time they woke and already the melting snow was dripping from the roof.

Dreep served them breakfast of tea and toasted muffins then told them, "Master Crook will see you as soon as you've finished breakfast."

Alice and Smiff looked at one another. "I thought you said Dreep was Master Crook?" Smiff whispered.

"Yes. Well? So what? Have you never been wrong, monkey-face?" she replied.

They went to the basement door and walked down the steep wooden stairway to a stone-floored room in the cellar. It was lit by a single mutton-fat candle. There were chairs facing the far wall and a curtain hung over the door in that wall.

The curtain rippled as the door opened. But no one stepped through the curtain. Instead a soft, deep voice spoke through it.

"You did well, Alice and Smiff. If this school did exams then you would have passed your first one. Bert is safe and retired, and the jewels will sell for enough money to help the poor people of Wildpool."

"It was a close shave at times!" Alice argued.

"I know. We cannot have you doing that every night. The police will get to know the way you work and will catch you in the end. No, you will only be sent out when we need your special skills," the voice said.

"So what do we do?" Smiff asked. "Sit round here all day?"

"No," the dreamy voice said. "You will have lessons but you will learn new ways to separate the rich from their money and help the poor. There are more crimes than burglary, you know."

Alice was excited by the idea. "Who says? You says? Like what?" she asked.

"Ah! You will have to wait and see."

"What do you mean when you said we have to 'separate the rich from their money'?" Smiff asked. "You made us give half back to Mayor Twistle."

"Mmmm!" Master Crook agreed. "They make their money from their land, their mines, their factories and their shops. But it is the poor who sweat to do the work. It is the poor who end in the workhouse when they are too old or sick or weak to work any more. The rich won't pay to look after the poor . . . even though it's the poor who made their fortunes for them. So Master Crook's pupils will . . . help them to pay. We can't take away all of their money . . . but let's take some. It's a sort of tax."

"I'm all for that," Alice said.

"But it is a dangerous business," Master Crook said and the soft voice had a hard edge to it now. "If they catch you their revenge will be terrible. I think we need a school trip to see the awful punishments they can give to the ones they catch! Perhaps we need a day in Darlham Gaol."

"School trip?" Smiff said. "Sounds interesting."

"Of course you will not spend all your time in the school," the voice said. "You, Alice, need to go back to your corner selling matches from time to time. I need you to report to me who is suffering there on the streets."

"Tell you who needs our help?" she said.

"Exactly. And you, Smiff, will go into the

mines, the shipyards and the factories to see who is suffering there. You are my eyes and ears in Wildpool."

"I can do that!" Smiff said eagerly. "But . . . I mean . . . Alice and I can't save the world on our own . . . no matter what your teachers teach us. The world is just too wicked!"

Master Crook sighed. "I know. Other pupils will join you. Each will bring some new skill. In fact Mister Dreep tells me there is a new classmate waiting to meet you right now. Go and make her feel welcome."

Chapter 12

ENDINGS AND STARTS

Constables Larch and Liddle stopped at the door to the police station before they went in. People were coming out on to the slushy streets to shop. The two constables bent their knees and spoke with one voice, as Inspector Beadle had taught them. "Mornin' all!"

They went inside and finished writing their report before they went home to sleep that morning.

WILDPOOL POLICE FORCE

REPORT ON THE TREASURE OF TWISTLE BURGLARY

DATE: 5th. January 1837

The above burglary has been solved. The criminal, Bert the Burglar, escaped justice but was driven from Wildpool, never to return. We have started to sweep the streets of Wildpool clean of the filth that fouls its gutters (as the mayor puts it). The streets of the town have now been cleaned of one burglar. His young assistants will not be able to operate without their leader. Plus a large quantity of silver was rescued. All in all a great result for the Wildpool police force

PC SEPTIMUS LIDDLE (PC 01)
PC ARCHIBALD LARCH (PC 02)

At 13 South Drive the fire was burning warm in the living room. Mayor Twistle stood with his back to the fire and polished his gold-rimmed spectacles on a silken handkerchief. His back was hot. But the heat in Arabella Twistle's brain burned hotter. "I have lost my jewels, Oswald, and you do not care."

The little man sighed. "Arabella, we took them from an old man in payment for a house we owned."

"It was a fair swap," the wide-chested woman stormed.

"It was a damp, worm-eaten cottage and the old man died within a year. When he died we took the cottage back. The jewels cost us nothing really," he smirked.

Lady Twistle leaned forward and prodded her husband with her fat finger. "I do not like to see crime go without punishment – crime and punishment go together like . . . like. . ."

"Like you and me, my sweet?"

"Like . . . birds of a feather. I want someone to pay for the theft of my jewels. I want someone to suffer."

"And so they shall, my dear. So they shall. I promise. In fact I made them suffer as soon as I got home last night. No one tangles with a Twistle and gets away with it."

Lady Twistle sat down quietly. "I am pleased to hear it, Ossie. Pleased."

The owner of Wildpool hardware shop was a happy man. He had checked his stock and found that someone had robbed him of a mop bucket that week. Maybe it had been that skinny boy with the ragged black hair, he thought.

Never mind. Sir Oswald Twistle's butler had just been into the shop to order a brand new, solid silver serving tray. That would make the shopkeeper, and the silver workers, enough money to get them through the winter. The thin old man, as grey as Smiff's blanket, turned a little bit pink with pleasure.

Alice and Smiff rose to their feet.

"Will we see you again?" Alice asked the curtain, then made a 'tut' sound. "Not that we're 'seeing' you now exactly!"

"When I need to tell you something . . .

or sometimes when you need to tell me something," Master Crook said.

"And will we ever get to see your face? Find out who you are?"

"Better not," the voice said. "For you will see me in the streets and theatres, taverns and town hall . . . anywhere in Wildpool. It would not be good for us to show that we recognize one another. Liddle and Larch are not the cleverest law officers in the world. But there are others who are more cunning and could catch us out."

"Like their Inspector Beadle?" Alice asked.

"He's a sly one is Beadle," Master Crook said softly. The curtain rippled and a door closed softly.

Alice walked towards it. "I want to see him. . ." she said.

"Leave it," Smiff said. "We just have to trust him. Sooner or later we have to trust someone." He looked at her. "After last night I know I can trust you."

Alice scowled at him. "I should think so too. I saved your life with my mop bucket idea!" Smiff's jaw dropped with shock that she could say such a thing.

"Let's go and see our new classmate," he said and led the way up the stairs to the classroom.

A girl in a poor black dress and shawl was turned away from them, looking out of the window at the gangs of men sweeping the snow from the streets so the fine carriages could slosh through the slush. She was about the same age as Smiff and Alice but her shoulders were broader. They seemed bent under the weight of a weary world.

She turned and her pale moon face smiled at the burglars, uncertain. "Hello again," she said.

"Nancy?" Alice gasped. "I thought you had a job as maid-servant to the Twistles."

Nancy nodded. "They threw me out when they lost the Twistle treasure. Lady Arabella said it was odd that someone picked the precious stuff and left the glass. She said it must have been someone who knew . . . someone like me."

"She couldn't prove anything," Smiff argued.

"She doesn't have to. She just sacked me – after she'd given me a beating. She wouldn't even give me a letter to get another job. I'd be on the streets without a penny . . . but Mr Dreep said he could help. He said I could learn a new trade here."

Dreep hurried into the room and rubbed his hands.

"So what trade are we going to learn?" Alice asked.

"We are going to learn highway robbery," Dreep said.

"That's an old one," Alice said.

"Ah, but we are going to invent a new way of using it. We are going to invent a completely new crime! When do you want to start?"

"As my old granny used to say, 'there's no time like the present'," Smiff grinned.

"Who says? You says?" Alice laughed. "I thought your granny said you can never have too many mop buckets?" she argued.

Smiff shrugged. "She said that too. You

never can have too many mop buckets . . . and I think we found out why last night!"

Alice nodded. "Right! No time like the present. Let's get started!"[52]

THE END

---

52 What a strange way to end a story, you cry. With a beginning. It isn't normal, I agree. But then, neither was Master Crook's Crime Academy.

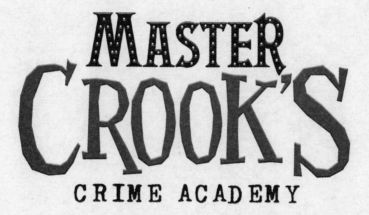

MASTER CROOK'S

CRIME ACADEMY

ROBBERY FOR RASCALS

Before word

YES, I REMEMBER 1837 AS CLEARLY AS IF IT WERE YESTERDAY. I KNOW! I KNOW, IT WAS SIXTY-FOUR YEARS AGO NOW. BUT I KEPT A DIARY AT THE TIME. I ALWAYS KNEW THAT I WOULD HAVE TO TELL THE STORY ONE DAY.

NOW THE OLD QUEEN IS DEAD. NOT BEFORE TIME, SOME MIGHT SAY. SHE CAME TO THE THRONE IN 1837 AND SOON AFTERWARDS THEY NAMED THE REST OF THE CENTURY AFTER HER. THE VICTORIAN AGE, THEY CALLED IT.

NOW SHE'S DEAD AND HER SON, FAT PRINCE EDWARD HAS BECOME KING EDWARD THE SEVENTH. I SUPPOSE THEY WILL CALL THIS THE EDWARDIAN AGE!

EVERYONE SAID THEY WERE SORRY TO LOSE OLD QUEEN VICTORIA. BUT THEY HAVE A FUNNY WAY OF SHOWING IT!. WE'VE HAD PARTIES IN THE STREET, BONFIRES WITH ROASTING POTATOES, FIREWORKS AND SWEETS FOR THE CHILDREN. I HAVE TO SAY, THERE HAS ALSO BEEN A LOT OF BEER FOR THE GROWN-UPS.

BUT WHY AM I TALKING ABOUT THE DEAD QUEEN AND THE NEW KING? WHAT I WAS TRYING TO SAY IS THAT I AM TURNING THE STRANGE STORY OF 1837 INTO A BOOK. I CAN TELL THE TALE NOW THAT WE ARE IN A NEW AGE AND NO ONE CAN BE HURT BY IT.

DO NOT ASK WHO I AM. I WON'T TELL YOU. BUT BELIEVE ME, I WAS THERE. I KNOW.

IT ALL HAPPENED UP IN THE BUSY, BLEAK, BLUSTERY AND BARBAROUS TOWN OF WILDPOOL, UP ON THE NORTH-EASTERN COAST OF ENGLAND. I LIVED THROUGH IT SO I KNOW THESE THINGS ARE TRUE. AMAZING . . . UNBELIEVABLE, EVEN . . . BUT AS TRUE AS I AM SITTING HERE SCRATCHING AWAY WITH MY FAVOURITE PENCIL.

YOU WON'T HAVE HEARD THIS STORY BECAUSE IT TOOK PLACE IN A POOR AND FORGOTTEN TOWN. I ALWAYS CALL WILDPOOL "A MIDDEN THAT'S HIDDEN".

I STARTED MY STORY IN JANUARY OF THAT FATEFUL YEAR.

BUT FEBRUARY HAD ITS OWN MYSTERIOUS TALE TO TELL. A TALE OF STEAMING, SCREAMING TRAINS AND TRACKS AND A VILE VILLAIN THAT ROBBED THE POOR TO MAKE HIMSELF RICH.

AT THE DARK HEART OF THE STORY IS MASTER CROOK'S CRIME ACADEMY. A SCHOOL THAT TEACHES THE TRICKS OF THE CRIMINAL TRADE TO THE YOUNG.

"SHOCKING!" YOU CRY. "WHAT A SCANDAL! A SCHOOL THAT TEACHES CHILDREN TO CHEAT, BOYS TO BURGLE AND GIRLS TO GURGLE! "[1]

"AHA! " I CRY. "ALL IS NOT WHAT IT SEEMS AT MASTER

---

1 I don't know why I said that. Does that ever happen to you? You are writing something sensible then your pencil runs off and writes something of its own? The girls in this story don't "gurgle". They do many curious things but gurgling isn't one of them. Can you forget I said that? Thank you.

CROOK'S ACADEMY. WAIT AND SEE. OR, AS THE SHIP'S CAPTAIN SAID WHEN HE THREW THE ANCHOR OVERBOARD . . . 'WEIGHT AND SEA'."

I WILL KEEP YOU WAITING NO LONGER. I TOLD YOU THIS STORY IS SET IN 1837. I MISLED YOU. (NEVER TRUST A WRITER.) IT REALLY BEGAN FORTY YEARS BEFORE THAT FATEFUL DATE. YEARS BEFORE THE OLD QUEEN WAS EVEN BORN. YEARS BEFORE I WAS BORN. THE YEARS WHEN OUR HUMBLE COUNTRY WAS AT WAR WITH FRANCE AND MIGHTY WARSHIPS WERE BUILT ON THE RIVER AT WILDPOOL.

SO, I WASN'T THERE MYSELF, BUT I HAVE SPOKEN TO A MAN WHO WAS THERE. WHO WAS A YOUNG MAN IN THE YEAR OF 1797 AT THE START OF OUR TALE. . .

A TALE OF FEAR, OF FORTUNE AND OF FUMBLE.

MR X[2]
28 FEBRUARY 1901

2 Writers who hide their name say they are writing under a "nom de plume". That 's French – and it is all right to use French since we beat them in that war. Anyway, "nom de plume" means "name of pen" . . . a name they only use when they are holding the writing tool. Since I don't use a pen I do not have a "nom de plume". I have a "nom de pencil".

Chapter 1

CARRIAGE
AND COURT

Wildpool Moor – 16th February 1797

The wind blew wildly across the moor and a young man shivered as he huddled in the bare bushes. His coat was thin and his boots more holey than a priest.

He wore a cloak and thought it made him look like the famous Dick Turpin. In fact the cloak was a grey blanket that he'd tied with a ribbon – it made him look like a scarecrow.

Cold mud seeped through the sole of his right boot. "I'm going to buy some new boots when I've done this robbery," he promised himself. It cheered him up. His pinched face suddenly glowed with joy. "And *socks*!" he moaned.

"I've *always* wanted a pair of socks. Oooooh! And stockings for my mum too. And a wig. . .[3]

. . . all the best highwaymen have a wig with a black hat with three corners. My name will bring terror to the roads round Wildpool, just as Dick Turpin's did in the south."

But his name would bring only laughter to the people of Wildpool. For his name wasn't Dick Turpin. It was Rick Turnip. He was almost the last of a long line of Turnips. Their roots went back into the mists of time.[4]

Fifty years before, Tom Turnip had been a terror. The Turnip families still had his picture on the walls of their cottages. They were proud of him.

He was a legend in the Turnip family. "Tom Turnip. The man they couldn't capture!"

That wasn't quite true. He was captured when he tried to escape from a tavern with a cheese sandwich. A cheese sandwich that he

---

3 A wig for him, not his mum, he should have said. His mother had enough hair. It flowed all the way down her back. None on her head, but plenty on her back.

4 That's a joke by the way . . . roots . . . turnip . . . see? I didn't say it was a good joke so don't groan like that.

hadn't paid for.

The law officer found our sandwich-stealing Tom hiding in a ditch; he put irons around his wrist and chained him to the village pump while he went to fetch the magistrate.

When the officer returned Tom Turnip's arm was still fastened to the pump . . . but Tom wasn't fastened to the arm. It was his false arm and he simply unfastened it and ran off.

Tom met his doom when he tried to cross the river on some slippery stepping stones and fell in. It's hard to swim with just one arm. . .[5]

. . .his body was washed out to sea and never seen again.

The Turnip family believed their Tom had escaped to America where he made a living robbing stagecoaches. That thought made them very happy.

The law officer handed the wooden arm back to the owner of the second-hand shop, so the shop-owner was happy too.

The Turnips said, "Tom was a dangerous outlaw."

---

5 Well, to be honest Tom had never learned to swim when he had two arms so he hand NO chance.

The law officer said, "No, he was 'armless."

THIS was the man that Rick Turnip has grown up hearing stories about. And stories are dangerous things. Rick wanted to BE Tom Turnip – highwayman.[6]

One night, in the Black Sheep Inn, he overheard the Twitch Family gang plotting an evil plot. "Tomorrow," they plotted, "Lord Fumble leaves Fumble Hall for his country house . . . Wishington Country Manor."

"So?"

"So whenever he goes from house to house he takes the Fumble Family Fortune with him on his coach."

"So?"

"So, we stop the coach, make him hand over the gold and make ourselves very rich!"

"How rich?"

"I just told you . . . very!"

Rick Turnip smiled a secret smile. He decided he would beat the Twitch Family at their own game and rob the coach before they

6 You will be delighted to hear he had no plans to copy Tom's bad habit of pinching ladies' bottoms. Just as well. He wasn't nippy enough! Hah! Pinch . . . nip . . . nippy? Geddit? Oh, never mind.

had the chance. He knew the rutted road Lord Fumble would take so all he had to do was hide in the bushes . . .[7]

Rick had no idea what time the coach would arrive. He was up at dawn and had waited all day without even a cheese sandwich to eat. He made his mouth go very watery, just thinking, "I wonder what happened to Tom Turnip's cheese sandwich that he nicked? I bet the law officer ate it!"

But as morning turned to afternoon he heard the clip-clop, clip-clop, clop-clop, flip-flop, clop-clip, flip-clip, flop-clop of carriage horses. (It was a very rutted road and that made it hard for the horses to clip and clop correctly.)

The carriage was the very latest 1798 model . . . even though the year was 1797, the carriage makers liked to boast it was next year's "model". That's how they sold it to their rich customers . . .

---

7 Which is where we had left him before you got me talking about old Tom Turnip!

BUY YOUR BRITAIN'S MOST WONDERFUL (BMW)

THE CLASSIC CARRIAGE

NEW 1798 MODEL OUT NOW FOR OUR BEST CUSTOMERS

2-door or 4-door models - extra wide for
ladies' dresses
2, 3 or 4 horse-power
Roof racks with built-in picnic hampers
Opening windows, 8-spoke wheels standard,
3 year or 300 miles warranty, Steel tyres,
Springs to soften the bumpiest roads.
PLUS free maps and driver's whip

The young man blew his nose on his handkerchief then fastened it round the lower half of his face.

He stepped out into the road and placed his finger under his grey cloak to make it look as if he had a gun.[8]

He raised his finger under the cloak. "Stand and deliver! Your money or your life!"

A shiver ran up through Rick Turnip's spine

8 Most highwaymen carried a pistol. Dick Turpin did. Rick Turnip didn't. Guns cost money. Once he'd robbed Lord Fumble he thought he'd go out and buy a pistol . . . after he'd bought socks, of course.

then back down again to where it started. "Ooooh!" he breathed. "I've always wanted to say that."

The coach stopped. The window slid down and the handsome young Lord Fumble stuck his handsome head out that was topped with a handsome hat. "What have we stopped for now, James?"

"Another highwayman, your grace," the driver said.

"Highwayman? Highwayman? Where's his horse?" the lord roared.

The driver turned to Rick. "His lordship wants to know where your horse is."

"I haven't got a horse!" Rick laughed in scorn. "I'm not made of money."

"He says he's not made of money . . ." the driver began to say.

"I heard! I heard, you ninny." The lord opened the door and stood on the step of the carriage. His suit was of finest blue satin with silver stitching and his socks were as white as snowdrops. "You can't be a highwayman without a horse, you rascal. You're a footpad.

Nothing but a common footpad. What are you? Well? What are you?"

"Erm . . . a footpad, my lord," Rick muttered miserably.

"Who do you think you are, calling yourself a highwayman? Who do you think you are? Eh? Dick Turpin?"

"No. Rick Turnip."

"Ah! Make a note of his name, driver. Rick Turnip, he says. We know your name. You may as well tell us where you live."

"I'm not telling you that! Do I look stupid?" Rick cried.

"How do I know if you look stupid if I can't see your face. You may have the most stupid face in the north for all I know."

"Well I haven't!" Rick cried and tore off the handkerchief.

"Jolly good, now we know what you look like. You'll be arrested. And I don't like footpads on my estate. I have them arrested and hanged, do you hear? Hanged! Drive on, driver!"

"Stop, put up your hands or I'll shoot!"

Rick called.

The driver dropped the reins and raised his hands.

The young and handsome lord pulled a blunderbuss from the coach. "That's what that bunch of ruffians down the road said," he explained. "But I shot first. And my gun was packed with all sorts of scrap metal. You should have seen them run, pulling bits of old candlesticks out of their backsides! Hah!"

Rick smiled slowly. "Ah! So it's not loaded now then, is it?"

Young Lord Fumble's handsome young face turned pale. "Ah . . . no . . . well. . ."

"So hand over the gold, please, or I shoot!" the footpad said politely.[9]

Lord Fumble threw the gun into the ditch and sighed. "Get the gold off the roof, driver, and hand it over. A bullet could do a lot of damage to my handsome face, you know."

9 To be honest it 's easy to be polite when you are pointing a gun at somebody. It is harder to be polite when (say) a stranger's dog bites your leg in the street. I mean, it is hard to say, "Excuse me, sir, but could I trouble you to remove your little pet 's teeth from my leg? It is rather uncomfortable." It is much easier to say something impolite like "*!***%!*%!%!*"

Rick Turnip's heart was fluttering like a wasp's wing. He was so near to being a hero like the family's famous Tom. So close to owning his first pair of socks. So close . . . and yet so far.

The Turnips have never been very lucky. So, at that moment, a gust of wind whipped at Rick's blanket-cloak and whisked it away from his pointing finger.

"Aha!" Lord Fumble said with a laugh like a donkey. "You haven't got a gun at all. You just have a finger. Driver . . . don't give this foul footpad a penny."

"But he'll shoot me!" the coach driver whined.

"With his finger?"

"You never know, my lord, the finger might be loaded," the man objected. "It's me that gets it if he's foot-padding around with a loaded finger!"

Lord Fumble frowned at Rick Turnip. "Is that a loaded finger you are pointing at my driver?"

"Well, to be honest, my lord, I couldn't

afford a gun OR the powder or the bullets."

"See, driver?" Fumble sneered. "You've been frightened by a finger. Now, arrest that man and we'll take him to Wildpool court, give him a fair trial, find him guilty and hang him."

Rick Turnip saw his plot going horribly wrong and decided it would be a good time to leave. He turned and began to creep towards the bushes. "Stop that man!" Lord Fumble cried.

A moment later the coach driver's whip flicked out and the thin leather wrapped itself around Rick's skinny neck. The driver hauled him back towards the coach, used some of the baggage rope to tie his hands then fastened it to the back of the coach.

Rick was forced to walk behind the coach to Wildpool and his fate. He stumbled over the February mud till at last they reached the courthouse. He was led to a cell and given some hot soup and fresh bread. It was the best meal he'd eaten. Ever.

After an hour Rick was led up to the court and chained to a screen that ran around a platform. This was called the "dock".

The clerk of the court was a fussy little man with spectacles and a bald head. "Court will rise for the judge!"

The few people who were in court stood up and a door behind the judge's bench opened. In walked the judge.

"Here!" Rick cried. "I've seen you before!"

"Silence in court," Judge Fumble growled. "What are the charges?"

"Armed highway robbery, your honour," the clerk said.

"Do you plead guilty?" Lord Fumble asked as he pushed the long horse-hair wig in place.

"Not really. I mean, I wasn't armed and I didn't rob nothing, did I?" the accused man shrugged.

"You tried to get money through menaces. That's a crime. You admitted it so you are guilty," Lord Fumble said.[10]

He reached under his desk and pulled out a black square of cloth. He placed it on

10 Oh, that sounds too, too harsh, doesn't it? But I have to tell you it is close to the truth. In 1833 a court report showed that most trials lasted just seven or eight minutes. The guilty were hanged within a couple of days. Some people now, in 1901, still call the 1830s "the good old days". Good for rope-makers maybe.

his head and read from a card with a black edge. "The court orders you to be taken from here to the place from where you came, and then to the place of execution, and that you be hanged by the neck until you are dead, and that your body be afterward be buried within the grounds of the prison in which you shall be held. And may the Lord have mercy on your soul."

Lord Fumble read it in a bored voice and stood up.

"Sorry, my lord," the clerk said quickly, "but you cannot hang a man for trying to get money with menaces."

"I can when it's me he was menacing," the judge said, in a menacing voice.

"The law won't allow it!"

Fumble sat down heavily. "What CAN I do to him then?"

"Forty days in prison, my lord."

He passed a sheet of paper to the judge who pulled a quill pen from an ink pot and scratched on the paper.

SENTENCE RECORD

His majesty's judge   *Lord Justice Fumble*

Has sentenced on this day   *16 February 1797*

The criminal known as   *Richard Turnip*

For the crime of   *demanding money with menaces*

The sentence being   *forty years' imprisonment*

Signed   *Fumble*

"Take him down," the judge ordered and passed the record card to the law officer who stood by the door.

"The court will rise!" the bald clerk cried quickly but Lord Fumble was out of the door before anyone could move.

And that is how Rick Turnip ended up in the great grey fortress that was Darlham Gaol, twenty miles south of Wildpool.

The governor of the prison sat at his desk

and read the "Sentence Record" when Rick Turnip had been delivered in the prison wagon. The governor blinked. He read it again. "Seems a bit harsh," he muttered. "Oh, well, the law is the law." He looked up at Turnip. "It seems you are going to be with us for forty years, my lad!"[11]

11 Did Lord Fumble make a mistake and write "years" instead of "days"? Maybe. Maybe not. I think this may just have been his cruel revenge. But what do I know? I wasn't there when Turnip went to prison. Of course I WAS there when he came out. And that's where he joins the story. . .

Chapter 2

COAL AND
CUSTARD

Wildpool Town – Tuesday 14th February 1837

Master Crook's Crime Academy was a large house, on Wildpool High Street. A warm coal fire crackled in the grate. Two of its three pupils sat at their tables waiting for lessons to begin.

Smiff Smith was a rough-haired, thin-faced boy with eyes as sly as a dog-snatcher in a poodle parlour full of puppies. He was drawing a poster. The girl at the other table was Alice White, a pinch-faced girl with curling fair hair and wild eyes.[12]

12 But she was not at all as twist-faced and cross-eyed as Smiff Smith's pictured showed. My Uncle Joseph's in-growing toenail wasn't as ugly as that. If Alice had seen the sketch Smiff would have had an in-growing nose. Know what I mean?

"What you doing, Smiff?" she asked.

He shrugged and hid the picture. "Just drawing a wanted poster for myself."

"What are you wanted for?" Alice asked.

"For being the most famous highway robber ever!" he said.

She scowled at him. "Have you ever tried highway robbery?" she asked.

"No . . . but that's what we're here for . . . to learn!" he said.

A tall man with gooseberry-green eyes that bulged a little entered the room. His thin moustache was stiff with wax but his fingers flowed like water in a fountain. "Good morning, class," he said.

"Good morning, Mr Dreep. Are you going to teach us how to be highway robbers?" Smiff asked. "Robbing stagecoaches? They're the crooks that get their names in the newspapers! And I want to be famous."

The teacher shook his head slowly. "They usually get in the newspapers because they are being executed. They've been caught."

"I wouldn't get caught!" Smiff argued.

"Who says, you says?" Alice jeered.

"Not if we learn from a real highwayman," Smiff answered. "What about it, Mr Dreep?"

"Hmm!" the teacher said and spread his rippling fingers. "Maybe Master Crook knows someone who will make a good teacher. I'll ask him. Meanwhile we'll get on with today's lesson ... stealing sausages to feed the old and helpless."

Smiff sighed. "I'll never get famous as a sausage stealer."

"And you may not end up on the gallows," Samuel Dreep told him. "Now ... step one ... first: Spot Your Sausage. .."

The February wind whistled wickedly through the town, just as it had forty years before when Rick Turnip had been arrested.

It was even colder in the home of Maximus Mixly. The tiny Mixly twins stood in front of the fire and gazed in wonder at a wooden frame on the mantelpiece.[13]

13 You are probably thinking this was a very dangerous thing to do. Children should not stand in front of a fire unless there is a fireguard in place. And you would be right ... usually. But this fire was made up of coal dust and glowed no warmer than a candle. They were safe, trust me.

> **THIS IS TO CERTIFY THAT MAXIMUS MIXLY IS THE OWNER OF ONE SHARE IN THE WILDPOOL AND HELTON RAILWAY TO THE VALUE OF ONE THOUSAND POUNDS**

"Yes, my children," Mrs Mixly said. "That is all our fortune. Your father paid everything we own and borrowed more from the bank to buy that!"

Millie looked at Martin and then at her mother. "Can we eat it?"

"No, my darling, it is far too precious to eat!"

"So when WILL we get something to eat, Mama?" Martin asked. He was a short, thin child with a face like a mouse.[14]

"It is dinner time at the Johnson house next door. Soon they will be finished. The cook will scrape the leftovers into the bin . . . and you, my darlings, can help yourselves."

"Thank you, Mama," Millie said with a sigh. She also had the face of a mouse. A very hungry

---

14 You know I mean it was a thin and pointed face with little bright eyes, like a mouse. I don't mean it was covered in grey fur and had long whiskers sticking out of the side of the nose. That would be plain ridiculous.

mouse. In fact if these children HAD been mice they would have not been afraid of cats. They were so hungry they would have eaten any cat that came near . . . whiskers and all.

"Mama," Martin said. "Could we not sell the paper in the frame for a thousand pounds. Then we could buy our own food and not have to eat it cold from the Johnsons' bin?"

Mrs Mixly shook her head sadly and stirred the coal dust till it smoked a little. "Lord Fumble has built the Wildpool and Helton Railway."

She pointed to a small map that lay on the table.

Mrs Mixly explained. "His lordship built it by selling a thousand shares at a thousand pounds a time . . . that is a million pounds. Think of that."

"Yes, but all we have is a piece of paper. Paper we can't even eat!" Millie moaned.

Mrs Mixly nodded. "The railway line runs from the coal mine at Helton to the coal ships on the river Wildpool," she explained. "It also has a branch line that joins Fumble Hall to Wishington Country Manor."

"I've seen the trains," Martin cried. "They

are beautiful. One day, when we are rich, I am going to buy a book and collect the numbers of the trains. I will be a trains-potter!"

Millie looked at him sourly. "Martin. There are only two trains on the line. Number 2 and Number 3.[15]

They won't take a lot of potting." She looked at her mama. "So we own a little bit of Wildpool and Helton Railway?"

"Yes, my dear."

"Which bit?"

"I . . . I don't know."

"Can't we SELL it and eat?"

"No one wants it. The railway is only used to carry coal. It only makes money for Lord Fumble," Mrs Mixly said. Millie opened her mouth to ask a question but her mama got in first. "But ONE day the line will join with the Great Northern Line . . . a railway line that will carry people from England to Scotland in a day. When Wildpool and Helton Railway

15 In case you are wondering what happened to Number 1 I have to tell you that, sadly, its boiler burst and it exploded. Engines did that a lot back in 1837. The explosion was a terrible loss to the trains-potters of Wildpool. It was an even greater loss to the engine driver's wife as her husband was blown into little pieces.

joins it then everyone will want to ride on the railway. Our one share will be worth TEN thousand pounds! We'll be rich! Rich! Rich, and all because of our precious share," she said dusting the wooden frame carefully with her handkerchief.

"I'd rather have an apple pudding," Martin muttered.

"With steaming custard," his sister added. "Come on, Martin, let's see what's in the bin next door."

Darlham Gaol – Wednesday 15th February 1837

The governor of Darlham Prison sat behind his desk. Old Rick Turnip stood in front of it.

"Good morning, Rick, how are you?"

"Very well, Charlie. There are some new books coming in the library today – a new one by that Walter Scott. I love his books. Lots of criminals like that Rob Roy and the Pirate. I read them all before I let the prisoners borrow them!" Rick chuckled.[16]

16 Rick Turnip was forty years older than when we left him in the courtroom, he was better fed and wore a neat uniform and strong boots. He even had socks – THREE pairs. It was a good life.

"We have had a visit from the famous Elizabeth Fry," the governor said. "You have heard of her?"

"Heard of her? Why, I've read her book *Prisons in Scotland and the North of England* many times. A great lady!"[17]

"Yes, well she has looked into some of the cases and showed a special interest in yours. It seems she was very angry that you've been locked away for forty years for a crime that was only worth forty days."

Turnip shrugged. "Not exactly *locked away*, Charlie. I mean, I learned to read, you gave me a wonderful job looking after the library, you send me out most days to buy your tobacco and newspaper. It's been a good life. I'm not complaining."

The governor was a flabby man in a slightly scruffy grey suit and dirty fingernails. He waved a grubby hand at Turnip now. "And we have loved having you. But your

17 You can still buy this book today. But it is not so exciting as a Master Crook's Crime Academy book. I am a very modest person. Really. But Elizabeth Fry was great at changing the cruel world of the old prisons. But she was not a great writer. I am.

sentence ends tomorrow. Mrs Fry has arranged for you to be released. You are free to go, Rick. A whole day early too! Isn't that good news?"

He passed a piece of paper across the table. Turnip read it. . .

DISCHARGE PAPERS

THIS TO CERTIFY THE CONVICT *Rick Turnip* HAS SERVED HIS SENTENCE AT DARLHAM GAOL. HE IS HEREBY RELEASED INTO THE WORLD. GOVERNOR CHARLES HOPE HAS GRADED THIS PRISONER AS *Class 1*

COMMENT: *Rick Turnip is the most honest convict I have ever met and a lovely bloke. I would trust him with my life. I hope someone will trust him with a job. He is a credit to Darlham Gaol.*

Charles Hope. 15 February 1837

The footpad frowned. His lips wobbled but it took a while for the words to come. "Go, Charlie? Go where?"

"Anywhere you want. Home!"

"But this is my home," the old convict said. "Mother died twenty years ago . . . you let me go to her funeral. But her house was just rented. I mean . . . I've nowhere else to go."

"Have you no family?" the governor asked.

"Mum had a brother that lived near to us in Wildpool. He's dead but he had children and grandchildren, I think. But I've never met them."

The governor reached into his pocket and pulled out some money. "In a way, Rick, you have been like a servant to me since I got here thirty years ago. I never paid you. . ."

"I never expected payment, Charlie. I was happy."

"No, but I feel it's my duty to lend you some money to set you on your way," the governor said. "Here are a couple of guineas. When you get yourself a job then you can pay me back."

Turnip picked up the money slowly. "Thanks, Charlie. You are all heart. All heart."

"Clear out your cell, we have a couple of sheep rustlers coming in this morning." The man stretched out a grubby and flabby hand. "Good luck, Rick. We'll all miss you. The way you looked after new criminals was marvellous. Helped them settle in, made them feel a bit less frightened. Yes. We'll miss you. Goodbye."

Turnip shook the governor's hand firmly. He sniffed away a tear and nodded goodbye.

An hour later the old highwayman was standing on the cobbles outside the prison gates and wondering which way to turn. He carried a small bundle with a blanket, a little food and his spare socks, his two guineas and a favourite book.

There was a small market in the town square that was a wriggling riot of noisy animals being bought and sold.[18]

A farm worker was struggling to load a pig on to his cart. Turnip hurried across to him, grabbed the back legs of the pig and hoisted it, squealing and kicking, into the old wooden cart.

The sweating farm worker had more mud and sweat on his face than the pig had on her whole body. He grinned and showed gaps where other pigs had kicked out his teeth.

18 The animals were not just noisy. They were also very smelly. Where there are animals there are animal droppings. If you ever go to a farm market be very careful where you put your feet.

"Thank you, mate. You're a brick. Anything I can do for you?"

"You could give me a ride," Turnip said.

"You don't know where I'm going."

"Neither do I," Turnip said with a shrug.

"I'm off to the piggery at Helton . . . five miles south of Wildpool. Do you know it?" the farm hand asked as he prodded the pony into life and creaked and clattered out of the market square.

"I haven't been to Wildpool for forty years. I think I may have family there," the ex-convict said. "It's as good a place to start a new life as anywhere," he said.

"A lot will have changed in forty years!" the driver chuckled. "You won't know the place."

For Rick Turnip, more had changed than he had imagined. He had heard about the railways in the newspapers and seen drawings of them. But when they neared Helton coal pits he saw one for the first time.

The cart stopped at a crossing and let a coal train roar through.

It was a fire-breathing monster, like

217

a mechanical dragon. The noise shook Turnip and drowned even the squeals of the frightened pig. He gasped as clouds of choking smoke swallowed the cart. "It's on fire! Quick! Put it out!"

"Nah! The fire heats the water and makes the steam. The steam drives the piston and the engine pulls the coal wagons."

"You seem to know a lot about these trains, my friend," Turnip said as he wiped the sooty smoke off his face.

"I do! I am a trains-potter. I pots the train numbers in my book."

"How many have you got?"

"BOTH of them!" the farmhand said proudly.

"There are only two?"

"Well, there were three till No. 1 blew up. But one day soon this line will join with the Great Northern Line and we'll see dozens. I'll be ready with me notebook when they come."

The pony pulled the cart over the track and the petrified pig stopped shaking.[19]

19 Of course, if the pig knew what was going to happen to her when she reached the butcher shop she would have been even more worried. But she had never heard of the dreadful word "bacon". And, if you ever meet a pig, it would be kinder not to tell them about butcher shops, ham sandwiches, chops and pork pies. If the pig asks you then it 's kinder to lie. Tell it porkies.

"Here we are!" the farmhand cried. "Helton Colliery."

Rick Turnip looked around and shivered. But it wasn't the February wind that chilled his bones.

Chapter 3

PUDDING AND POLICEMEN

Wildpool Town – Wednesday 15th February 1837

Mrs Mixly looked at a sign hanging on a green gate.

She was pale as a February frost and looked as worried as a cat in a dogs' home. She rapped at the door. After a minute the door was opened by a boy with a shining face and spiked dark hair. "Hello, madam. Master Crook's Crime Academy at your service."

The woman threw a worried glance over her shoulder, cleared her throat and spoke quickly.[20]

"I wonder if I could see Master Crook ... or do I need an appointment?"

The boy pulled a face. "I can ask ... but you can't see him. Nobody sees him. I've been here a month and I haven't seen him yet. I've spoken to him a few times though."

"How do you do that if you can't see him?"

"I either talk down the speaking tube. Or if he has a tricky job for me he sometimes tells me about it down in the cellar – it's dark and he's behind a curtain."

"How strange!"

"He's a strange man ... but brilliant! Come this way," the boy said and led the way into the house. "My name's Smiff, by the way. Who shall I say is calling?"

20 You should be very careful to look before you throw anything over your shoulder. Someone may be standing behind you and they could be seriously hurt. Especially if it 's a horseshoe. Throwing a horseshoe over your left shoulder is lucky. But unlucky for someone walking behind. Being hit by a worried look is not so painful.

"Mrs Mixly," the woman said.

Smiff led the way into a pleasant living room with comfortable chairs. A girl was dusting ornaments. She was a moon-faced, pleasant girl.[21]

"Nancy," Smiff said. "Would it be a lot of trouble to make Mrs Mixly a cup of your best tea?"

"It would be a pleasure, Smiff," the girl smiled and glided silently out of the room like a good maid-servant would. Nancy was a pupil at the Crime Academy, of course, but she used to be a maid to the Mayor of Wildpool, Sir Oswald Twistle, and she had loved her work . . . till the mayor and his wife had thrown her on to the snow-covered streets.

Smiff went across to a tube that hung on the wall by the window. He pulled a cap off the end and blew down the tube. He placed the tube to his ear and, after a few moments, grinned, "We're in luck. Master Crook is in his office." The boy spoke down the tube and explained about Mrs Mixly. Then he put the

21 I don't want to be unkind but she was also rather "dumpy". Some people are just born that way and Nancy was one of those people.

tube back to his ear and listened, nodding.

Finally he pushed the cap back on the tube and turned back to the visitor. "Master Crook will see you now . . . ah, here's Nancy . . . let me take your cup of tea downstairs for you! But leave your handbag here."

"My handbag?"

"We have to be careful. Master Crook has enemies. We can't risk someone taking a weapon into the room and hurting him, can we?"

"I suppose not," she said and placed the bag on the table by the door.

The boy led the way to a door, opened it and went down some dimly lit steps. At the bottom was a small room with just a chair and a small table facing a curtain. Smiff left and as Mrs Mixly sipped at her tea a slight draught ruffled the curtain. A door had opened behind it. There was a creak, as if a large man had sat down in a chair.

Master Crook's voice was deeper than the North Sea when the tide is in but warmer than the summer sands (when the tide is out, of course). "Good day, Mrs Mixly. How can I help?"

The woman took a deep breath. "I want you to teach my little twins how to make a life on the street. . . I did think they might make beggars, but the new police force would whip them and send them home. I thought your sign says you can do it without them being caught by the police?"

"Ah, the Wildpool police force . . . Constable Liddle and Constable Larch. Yes, stern upholders of the law. And, of course, their stout Inspector Beadle. But tell me, why would you want the poor children to beg? You are well dressed. You live in a large house and your husband has a good job in the shipping offices making ten shillings a week."

"How do you know all that?" the woman breathed.

"Master Crook's Academy has files . . . we study the town and its people. It's one of the jobs the students have been doing since we opened. We don't spend every day with classes and crimes, you know. We gather facts and store them up. You never know when you may need a good juicy fact," the warm voice gurgled.

"Yes, my Albert has a good job ... but all the money goes to pay the bank for the money we borrowed. The money to pay for a share in Lord Fumble's railway," she said and pulled out a handkerchief to dab at a sniffle.[22]

For the next ten minutes the story poured from her as freely as her tears. She had held those tears back when she spoke to her husband and the children. But something about Master Crook's cosy room and gentle voice made her rush and gush out her troubles.

At the end Master Crook said softly, "I have heard of other cases like this. There are many families who have suffered from Lord Fumble's little scheme."

"So you'll take the twins? You'll teach my Martin and Millie?"

There was a sigh from behind the curtain. "No."

---

22 That happens, doesn't it? Writers say tears run down when someone cries. But the truth is snot runs down at the same time. They like to say, "The woeful woman wept! " That is more pleasant than saying, "The sad lady snotted."

"Ah!" Mrs Mixly cried. "But your sign promises. . ."

"Hush, my dear lady, and listen a moment. There are a hundred families in Wildpool alone who are in your sad scrape. The answer is not to send all the children on the streets to beg. That is not the Master Crook way. No, the answer is to deal with the problem. And the problem is Lord Fumble. Can you hold out just a week longer?"

"We've got by for two months now . . . though it was the poorest Christmas those children could ever wish to see."

"In a week I may have found a way to get your money back. One week."

The woman rose to her feet and began to climb the stairs. In the room above, the cap in the end of the speaking tube sounded a whistle. Smiff hurried across and listened. Then he dropped the tube, ran to a drawer in a cabinet, pulled out a purse and found two golden sovereigns. He picked up Mrs Mixly's purse and dropped the coins in.

When the woman appeared at the doorway

from Master Crook's cellar he was holding the open bag. "What are you doing?" she cried.

"Searching for a weapon," the boy said quickly. "It's a rule of the Academy. But there's no weapon there . . . oh, and we may be criminals but we don't steal from visitors!"

She shrugged. "I have nothing to steal."

Smiff gave a great laugh. "Hah! You have two gold pieces!"

"I haven't!" the woman argued.

Smiff pulled them from the bag, held them up to the light then dropped them back in. "You have now."

He handed the bag to Mrs Mixly. The woman wandered out into the February afternoon in a daze. "Apple pudding tonight for my little dears. Apple pudding . . . and custard!"

Back in the house Smiff grinned at Nancy and winked. Nancy's moon face glowed warm as the sun.

Helton Colliery – Wednesday, 15th February 1837

Helton Colliery sprawled like a black slug over a hill and a valley. Great grey mounds of slimy rock had been dumped on the earth like mini-mountains of waste. Huge wooden wheels on iron towers whirred and wound ropes that took men under the ground to carve the coal. Then they wound the other way to pull up trucks of rich and shining coal.

Steam pumps belched water from the workings into a rusty stream that had once been as clear as a tadpole's tail, but the poisoned tadpoles were long dead now.

Rattling belts carried the coal on overhead lines to railway trucks and filled them ready for the locomotives to carry them down to the docks at Wildpool.

Miserable men and grey-faced women trudged through the cold puddles; no one spoke and no one smiled.

"You could get a job here, old-timer," the farmhand said. "They're always looking for strong men."

Rick Turnip looked around the scene as bleak as the dark side of the moon. "I have a job," he said proudly.

"What's that then?"

"I'm a highwayman . . . or I was before I spent a little time in Darlham Gaol. I robbed coaches. I'm from a long line of famous highwaymen!"

"Dick Turpin?"

"No . . . Rick Turnip."

The farmhand smirked and smothered a laugh. (They all did that.) "Well," he said, "you'll find the great people of the land hardly use carriages any more. They build railways and have their own railway carriages. Even stagecoaches are rare now."

Turnip climbed down from the cart and shook hands with the farmhand. "Thank you, my friend. I'll walk the rest of the way to Wildpool."

"Best of luck with the highway robbing – some of those rich people need to share it around a bit."

Rick Turnip nodded then turned his face to the cold north wind and followed the road that ran alongside the railway track. "Yes, I have a job," he said to himself. "Highwayman." There was a spring in his step as he left the ugly Helton valley behind and saw the smoking chimneys of Wildpool ahead.

To his right the sea was whipped white and green by the wind. Coal ships were coming and going up the river to dock at Wildpool quaysides and load up with the coal from the mines.

Locomotive No. 3 smoked and coughed its way up to the ridge. The trucks were empty but it was still quite a climb. A man stood in the doorway of a tiny hut by the track wearing a heavy black overcoat and carrying two flags, a red and a green. "Good afternoon!" he called to Rick Turnip as he passed him on the road.

"Good afternoon. Waiting for the train?"

"No. I'm a policeman," the man explained

"A law officer?"

"No, no, no! Not that sort of policeman. It's the name the railway companies give to track guards. Our job is to stop trains running into one another. We wave flags. Important job but not policemen like Constable Liddle and Constable Larch in Wildpool . . . they are part of the new police force. Very confusing, but don't worry. I can't arrest you! Hah!"

"Good," the ex-convict muttered and hurried down the hill towards the chuffing train. "What can a highwayman do when there's no coaches and carriages to rob? Why, rob a train, of course!"

The railway policeman was out of sight. The old footpad felt a thrill of excitement as he took out his handkerchief, blew his nose then tied it round the bottom half of his face.[23]

He took a blanket from the bundle he was carrying and quickly threw it over his shoulder. "Just like Dick Turpin," he chuckled.

The footpad raised his fingers under the cloak so it looked as if he were carrying a pistol.

The pounding pistons of the train came closer. Rick Turnip stepped forward till he was almost touching the track. The mighty metal monster pulled level with him, engine roaring, pistons hissing, wheels clanking, steam spitting. Turnip had trouble hearing his own voice as he cried, "Stand and deliver, your money or your life . . . ooooh! I do love saying that again!"

23 I wish he wouldn't do that. Why can't he have two handkerchiefs? One to blow his nose and one to wear as a mask. Blowing your nose on your mask is . . . well, it makes me a little sick to think about it.

The driver stood on the platform behind the boiler. His fireman shovelled coal into the firebox. They heard nothing apart from their metal dragon's roar. They saw an old man by the side of the track, wearing a handkerchief and a blanket. The whooshing steam blew the blanket away from Turnip's hand and left him pointing a finger at the men on the locomotive.

The train roared on and the empty coal trucks clattered past. The driver turned to his fireman. "Who was that?"

"Dunno," the fireman said. "Probably one of those trains-potters."[24]

24 Now here's a strange thing . . . well, it seems strange to me. Maybe your life is so weird that nothing seems strange . . . not even a pink and purple parrot on your pillow. I don't know.

But I found it strange that Master Crook set up his Crime Academy next door to the Wildpool Police Station.

Chapter 4

GOLD AND GUARDS

Wildpool Town – Wednesday 15th February 1837

Wildpool Town, and its mayor Sir Oswald Twistle, were extremely proud of their new police force in 1837.

There were three officers in that first year. In charge was the mighty Police Inspector Beadle. His office was in the basement of the police station and some people believed he lived there. From time to time he came upstairs into the police station and when he did the stairs trembled as if an elephant was walking up them. In fact an *elephant* would tremble if it saw Police Inspector Beadle because the elephant would feel small.

That February morning the stairs trembled. The two constables, Liddle and Larch stood to attention.

A maid polished the desk and a mop stood in a bucket by the door. The whole place shone and smelled of beeswax polish. The maid could see her face in the shining desk top. It was a sharp face with blue eyes like a doll and topped by curly fair hair.

Beadle waddled in and stood behind his desk. He sat in a chair that was as wide as a sofa. "Be seated, men." He turned to the girl. "Alice . . . go and clean the kitchen."

"Done it, sir."

"Then do it again. This is a private meeting with secret matters to discuss. Go!" he said and the voice was deep and menacing.

Alice went.

The constables dropped into two hard wooden chairs. How can I describe these two fine law men to you? I won't try. Here's what Police Inspector Beadle wrote in his first report.

> Liddle is thin, ancient and not very
> bright.
> Larch is heavy, slow and as bright as
> a dark lantern.

Beadle passed them a sheet of paper.

WILDPOOL POLICE FORCE
INSTRUCTIONS

DATE: 15 February 1837

PC Septimus Liddle (PC 01) and PC Archibald Larch (PC 02) are hereby assigned to guard duty on the Wildpool and Helton Railway Special Train. On Monday 27th February at 3:00 p.m. the constables will report to Fumble Hall. A large quantity of gold is to be loaded on to Lord Fumble's private carriage. Locomotive No. 2 will divert from coal-hauling duties to pull this train. The train will go to Wishington Country Manor where it will be unloaded. Constable Liddle and Larch will not let the Fumble Fortune Carriage out of their sight until the money is safely stored in the safe at the Manor.

POLICE INSPECTOR BEADLE

Constable Larch asked, "But who will guard Wildpool while we are rushing off on train duty?"

Police Inspector Beadle nodded, "I shall."

Constable Liddle frowned. "Are we supposed to work for private persons . . . I mean Lord Fumble can hire his own bodyguards."

"He could . . . but the mayor promised Lord Fumble that the mighty Wildpool police would take on this task. It is a large amount on money and the future of Wildpool Railway depends on it. And the future of Wildpool depends on the railway. The railways are spreading across the land like roots from a mighty tree. Every town that is connected to it will grow. Every town that is not connected will wither and die."

"I see," Liddle said . . . though he didn't.

Larch smiled happily. "I always wanted to ride on one of those train things. I've heard Lord Fumble's carriage is like a room in his house . . . seats covered in velvet, cabinets full of wine and a stove to warm it and to make him nice hot tea."

"You will be riding in the guard van behind," Inspector Beadle sighed. "It's more like a room in Darlham Gaol ... wooden benches, no wine and very cold. But the Wildpool police force are happy to suffer a little discomfort for the honour of guarding the Fumble Fortune."

"Are we?" Liddle asked, a little miserable.

"We are," Beadle said. He slapped his massive hands on the desk and pushed himself to his feet. "But over the next week we have to work at the road safety campaign we talked about last week."

"Oh, sir, do we have to?" Larch groaned. "I got a terrible battering yesterday."

"It was your own fault," Liddle smirked. "The road safety campaign says you have to help old ladies to cross the road, keeping them safe from horses, carriages and carts."

"I did that! I got Dame Winter all the way across without even a splash of mud."

"Yes," Liddle reminded him, "but Old Dame Winter didn't want to cross the road, did she?"

"No," Larch sighed. "She battered me with her umbrella."

Beadle simply shook his large head and left the room to go back to his office in the basement.

"Come on then, Larch," Liddle said tucking his instructions into his notebook. "Let's go and help children across the road from Dame Winter's School. At least the children don't batter you with umbrellas."

"But one of them gave me a nasty bite on the kneecap last week!" Larch argued as he followed Liddle out of the room . . . leaving his copy of the instructions on the wooden chair.

Silence. Click! The door opened. Alice slipped into the room. She saw the paper on the seat and picked it up. She read it. She smiled. The girl folded it and ran across to the door. She took a dark cape from a peg to keep out the February wind then hurried out of the door into the street.

Evening dark came early in Wildpool winter and the lamp-lighter was wandering down the streets turning on the gas-green glow to brighten the smoky streets.

"Evening all!" Liddle and Larch called as they passed him.

Alice White didn't go very far. She made sure Constables Liddle and Larch had plodded around the corner then she turned into a gateway of the building next door – the one marked with a red sign that said, "Master Crook's Crime Academy".

An old man was standing at the front door talking to the boy Smiff. Smiff saw Alice coming up the path, tugged the old man inside and said, "Hello, Alice. What's new?"

She waved the police report in front of him. "This! Wait till Master Crook sees this!" She smiled at the old man. "Hello. You must be one of the new teachers Mr Dreep told us about."

"No . . . I . . . er . . . who's Mr Dreep?"

"Our teacher . . . Master Crook's assistant." Alice lowered her voice and muttered, "Some of us think Mr Dreep may be Master Crook just pretending to be Mr Dreep and that

Master Crook isn't himself except when he's pretending to be himself. See?"

"No."

"That way, if we ever get caught and the police try to arrest Master Crook, we can always say we have never seen Master Crook . . . which none of us has, unless Mr Dreep is really Master Crook in which case we have seen him but we can't swear in court we've seen him because we didn't know we were seeing him when we saw him if you see what I mean?"

"No . . ."

"It all makes perfect sense," she shrugged.[25]

"So what are you going to teach us?" she asked eagerly. "NOT that I'm in school at the moment, of course. I'm working next door as a maid and really I'm a—"

"Alice!" Smiff cried. "This gentleman is a stranger. We know nothing about him. You can't go blabbing our secrets to a stranger."

25 And of course it DOES make perfect sense, doesn't it? Especially if you're a person potty enough to have a pink and purple parrot on your pillow. If it doesn't make sense then I have just one thing to say to you . . . Ask your parrot to explain.

"Who says? You says?" she asked angrily. Alice turned to the stranger. "You look like a criminal to me," she said.

"Do I? Why thank you, young lady. I come from a great criminal family ... a family of highwaymen!"

"Here!" Alice cried. "I told you he was our new teacher! Mr Dreep said our next big crime would be highway robbery, didn't he? Well?"

"He did," Smiff nodded.

"But ..."

"Alice will take you to Mr Dreep."

"Who says? You says?" Alice exploded. "Take him yourself. I'm off to see Master Crook. I have some very important business with him." She walked across the room and blew down the message tube.

Smiff shrugged his skinny shoulders. "Come into the kitchen. Mr Dreep's making us some supper. Want some?"

He led the way out of the classroom and down the corridor to a warm room where a fire glowed. Kettles and pots hung from the mantel-shelf and some bubbled and spat over the fire with the rich taste of best beef soup.

A tall man stirred the pot. He smiled as Smiff entered. The man had a fine, white smile under a thin, dark moustache. He would have been handsome but for his eyes that bulged just a little like pale gooseberries. His shirt was as fine and white as his smile and the sleeves were rolled up as he worked.

"Good evening, my friend. Can I help you to some soup? You look as if you could do with a good meal."

"I've lived on bread and water for forty years," the old man said.

"You'll eat well here, never fear. We look after our teachers like lords," Dreep said. He wiped his hands on a towel and stretched out his right hand to shake the old man's. "Samuel Dreep at your service. And you are?"

"Rick Turnip, sir."

"From the famous Turnip family of highway robbers? What an honour to meet you, sir! Why, children still sing songs of your famous Tom Turnip as they skip and play ball games," Dreep laughed. He pulled a book from a shelf. "Here's a collection of street rhymes . . . look!"

Tommy Turnip

Tommy Turnip caused alarm
Bandit robber with one arm.
Wildpool called him nasty curses
Cos he nicked the women's purses

Tommy Turnip roamed the streets
Stealing little children's sweets
Tommy Turnip, law men got 'em
When he pinched a lady's bottom

Tommy Turnip came to harm, he
Got caught pinching someone's sarnie
Tommy threw his arm away,
Lived to rob another day.

Tommy Turnip is no good
Chop him up for fire wood
If the fire won't burn his head
Use his wooden arm instead.

Dreep shook the old man's hand. "And of course *you* are just as famous!"

"I am?"

"Oh, yes. Master Crook still talks about the great wrong that Lord Fumble did to you. What was it? Forty years in prison?"

"Yes, sir, forty years," the old man sighed. "But they weren't too bad. In fact I had some happy times," he added. "The best bit was showing the new criminals the ropes!"

"The hangman's ropes?" Smiff gasped.

"No . . . it's a saying. Showing someone the ropes – teaching them how to get along in the prison. I miss that," he said softly.

Dreep rubbed his thin, white hands. "But now you are here you have a whole future of teaching our students about highway robbery. Master Crook will be so pleased to see you."

"Well, that's the thing, sir," Rick Turnip said. "I didn't come here to *teach* . . . I came here to learn. Lord Fumble caught me when I tried to rob his carriage all those years ago. These days they have railway engines instead of coaches. I haven't a clue how to rob one of those things! I tried earlier today. I ended up looking a real prawn."

Dreep stirred the soup and began to spoon it out into a bowl. He placed it on the table with fresh, crusty bread he'd baked earlier in the day. "Mr Turnip, you rob a train in the same way you rob a carriage."

"How?" the old man asked, sniffing at the soup and dipping in a piece of bread.

"You're the greatest highwayman Wildpool has ever seen. YOU tell ME!" Dreep said.

Turnip sucked on the bread and let the soup warm him from the inside as the fire warmed him on the outside. In Darlham Gaol he had forgotten what warm was. "First, you have to stop it," he said.

"Exactly!" Dreep clapped.

"But I don't know how to stop a railway engine," the old convict moaned.

"Neither do I," Smiff said. "But at Master Crook's Crime Academy it's our job to find out."

"I see," the old man said, his heart growing warm at the thought that he was among friends.

"And THEN you need to find a train worth robbing," Dreep said.

"Stop it, rob it, job done."

"I will look at the business of stopping a moving train," Dreep said.

"And Master Crook will tell us when and where there will be a train worth robbing!" Smiff finished.

"How will he do that?" Rick Turnip asked.

"He has his ways," Smiff said wisely.

As the fearless three were in the kitchen plotting, Alice was in the cellar below passing a paper through the curtain to Master Crook.

There was a long pause with just the soft rustle of paper. Finally Master Crook's low voice said, "You have done well, young Alice. Now take the paper back to where you found it – if they think their plan has been stolen the police will suspect you and sack you. They will also change their plan."

"That's good thinking that is!" Alice chuckled.

"We have just one week to work out how to rob a train."

"I've heard of highway robbery but never a

train robbery," Alice said.

"Then the students of Master Crook could be about to pull off the world's first train robbery!"

"Great," Alice said. "I like the sound of that."

"And one last thing," Master Crook crooned softly. "Give Nancy a message. She will meet the old man who's just arrived, his name is Turnip. I do not want her to tell him her name – her family name. Understand? And hurry."

"What is her name? Why shouldn't she tell him?"

Suddenly the Master's voice grew loud enough to make the curtain tremble. "You ask too many questions, Alice White. Do as I say or you'll be back on the streets selling matches."

Alice glared at the curtain. "Who say? You says?" she said. But she said it very, very quietly.

Chapter 5

A RAT AND
A RAILWAY

Wildpool Town – Wednesday 15th February 1837

Nancy showed Rick Turnip to a large, airy room on the upper floor of the Crime Academy. "Here you are, Mr Turnip. Your bedroom."

The old man looked around, worried. The wide windows looked out over Wildpool. It was a clear night and a three-quarter moon glowed in the frosty sky. The school stood on the road overlooking the river. Bright lights shone in the shipyards where men worked through the night to build ships. Gas street-lamps sparkled over the frost-dusted cobbles.

A few carts skidded along the roads,

shivering men and women hurried towards the taverns. Stray dogs sniffed for rats in the dark alleys. Stray cats watched from the tops of black-brick walls. The rich rode warm in their carriages to the theatre, wrapped in fat furs.

"I'm not used to this," the old man said.

"I've made up a lovely comfortable bed for you with fresh sheets and warm blankets. The mattress is stuffed with goose-feathers."

The ex-convict shook his head. "I don't think I could sleep in that," he said. "Sorry, but I've spent forty years sleeping on a board with just a blanket. No lights and just the sound of men moaning."

Nancy nodded. "Why not sleep on the floor then," the chubby girl said kindly. "I'll pull the curtains so the light doesn't come in. Sorry I can't do the moaning men."

"You're a good girl. What's your name?"

"Nancy, sir."

"Nancy what?"

The girl turned even paler than usual. "I'm not supposed . . . I mean . . . I'm just Nancy, sir."

"Thank you, Just Nancy!" the old man smiled. "It's not my old cell in prison, but I'm sure I'll be happy here."

Nancy bobbed a clumsy curtsey, the way she used to do when she was a maid to the mayor. She took the candle and closed the door, leaving the old man in darkness.

Wildpool Town – Thursday 16th February 1837

The next morning the students at Master Crook's Crime Academy sat at the tables in the teaching room. They had maps and sketches of the Wildpool and Helton Railway as well as blank paper and pencils to make notes. Samuel Dreep stood at the front of the class with Rick Turnip and rubbed his thin hands together.

Alice, Smiff and Nancy looked at their teachers eagerly.[26]

"Students, may I first welcome the famous,

26 Yes, this is a really weird thing. Children who ENJOY school! Since 1870 children have been FORCED to go to school. You are probably one of them, poor thing. Rick Turnip had forty years locked away all day, just as you school pupils are . . . but at least no one forced him to listen to a boring old teacher droning like a bee and stinging with his cane like a wasp. Schools? They're a crime. But NOT Master Crook's.

the infamous, the incredible Mr Rick Turnip!" Samuel Dreep cried. The class cheered and clapped while the old convict blushed. "This great highwayman robbed the rich single-handed."

"Erm," Rick interrupted. "I think you are thinking of Tom Turnip . . . he was single-handed cos he only had one arm."

For a moment Dreep was flustered. "Quite . . . yes . . . as I was saying . . . this man robbed Lord Fumble without any help from anyone. And now, forty years later, he is going to do it again!"

Cheers.

"Am I?" Turnip asked.

"Why, yes. The train we are planning to rob is Lord Fumble's train with Lord Fumble's fortune on board. This was the man who had you locked away for forty years!"

Smiff jumped to his feet. "Revenge time!"

"Oh, I'm not interested in revenge," the old highwayman sighed.

Smiff sat down suddenly. But Nancy jumped to her feet. "You're right, Mr Turnip. This is not about you and Fumble. This is about saving the families Fumble cheated. Saving them from starving! This is about people like the Mixly family. This isn't revenge . . . it is justice!"

The girl raised a fist above her head. Smiff and Alice looked at her in silent awe.

"Thank you, Nancy," Dreep said with a faint smile on his face. "I can see you have taken Master Crook's ideas into your heart." Nancy sat down. Dreep turned to Alice and took a deep breath.[27]

"What you did yesterday with the police note was wonderful work. . ."

Alice glowed with pride then felt Mr Dreep was going to say "but. . ."

"But," he said carefully. "We need you back inside the police station. You are our eyes and ears in that place. The more you can learn about the enemy the easier it'll be to defeat them."

"Awwww!" the girl groaned. "I wanted to do the robbery!"

---

27 The sort of deep breath you would take just before you stepped into a cage with a man-eating lion . . . or even a woman-and-child-eating lion. You take a deep breath for courage. And what do you get? Courage? No, you get air.

"I know you did, Alice, but we each have a job to do and spying is your job."

Alice stuck out her bottom lip and decided to be awkward for the rest of the lesson . . . which she was.

The Mixly twins were excited.

"Daddy! Daddy!" they cried.

Mrs Mixly slapped a hand on the breakfast table. "Really, Martin and Millie, you must not make a fuss at the breakfast table! It is bad for your father's stomach. He must eat his food in peace."

"But . . ." Millie moaned.

"I said NO, Millie Mixly, and that means No." She placed a pie in the middle of the table.

The twins sat in silence supping their porridge as their father carved into the pie and tucked into it hungrily. "It's a long time since we had any meat in our meals, Mrs Mixly," he said happily. "Where did you say this pigeon came from?"

"The cat brought it in, Mr Mixly," she said.

"And jolly tasty it is too," he said, mopping the gravy with a morsel of bread.

"But—" Martin began.

His mother raised an eyebrow and he fell silent.

Mr Mixly wiped his mouth on a napkin then rose to his feet. "Time I was off to the bank. I'll work all the better with that pigeon pie inside me."

"That's what I thought," his wife said.

The man put on his tail coat and top hat then wrapped a scarf around his neck to keep out the Wildpool winter wind. He picked up a leather case full of papers and went to the front door. "I'll be working till midnight to make some extra money," he said.

"Again?" Mrs Mixly said, shaking her head. "You're a good man."

"And I have a good wife, feeding me like that." He stopped and smiled down at the children. "Now, you two rascals, what were you trying to tell me?"

Millie looked at Martin. Martin looked at Millie. "We were going to tell you, the cat brought in a fat pigeon," the girl said.

"I think I know!" their father cried smacking his lips. "Be good. See you tomorrow." He stepped out of the door and strode up the street.

Mrs Mixly frowned. "Your father will have proper food tonight. I can go shopping with the money I found after my visit to Master Crook's Crime Academy. No more pigeons that the cat dragged in."

Martin looked at Millie. "It was a funny-looking pigeon that the cat caught," the boy mumbled. "It looked like a very fat rat to me."

Millie gave him a bright smile. "If Father wants to think it was a pigeon then let him," she said. "Better that way."

Martin nodded. "Much better."

"Now, class," Dreep was saying to the Crime Academy class. "Mr Turnip has already told us the first part of any highway robbery is to stop the carriage. That was easy with the old horse-drawn coaches. You just scared the driver into stopping the horses," the teacher explained and pointed to a picture on the blackboard.

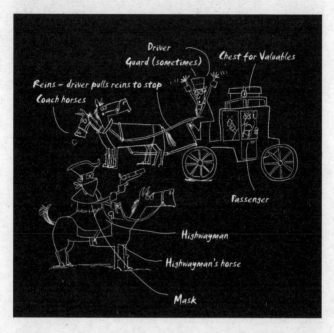

"Now we have a railway locomotive instead of horses. These things travel at up to forty miles an hour. They are past you before you can blink," Dreep went on.

"As I found out yesterday," Turnip tutted.

"The driver even has a wind shield he can hide behind if a robber pointed a gun," Dreep went on and showed another picture.

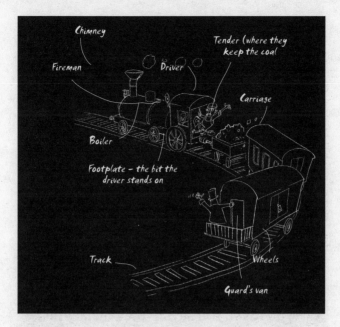

"No one can stop *that*!" Alice snorted . . . being awkward and unhelpful.

A slow smile spread over the face of the old highwayman. "Ah, but you are wrong, young Alice. Someone can stop it."

"Who says? You says?"

"The *driver* can stop it!" the old man said quietly.

"Oh, yeah, well, of course, I know that!" she said angrily. "But none of us is driving the treasure train, are we?"

"Why not?" Smiff said suddenly. "Mr Turnip is a genius! We always knew he was. One of us drives the train and stops it in a quiet spot."

"Hah!" Alice sneered. "Not only can you not drive a train, master smarty Smiffy, but they wouldn't let you. Caw, I've eaten pork pies with more brains than you got."[28]

"And I've seen pork pies that are prettier than your face," Smiff said, rising to his feet.

"You won't be eating pork pies, Smiff, you'll be swallowing your teeth if you don't watch it!" she raged.

"Who says? You says?" the boy laughed.

"Here! You can't say that! I say that!" Alice roared and Nancy had to grip her wrists to stop her lashing out at Smiff.

Dreep looked on and did nothing to stop the fight. "Smiff can be very irritating, can't he, Alice?"

"You're telling me. I wish I didn't have to share a room with the little mongrel," she snapped.

---

28 This is gruesome but true–some. Pork butchers in Wildpool were not too fussy about what they put in their pies. If they slipped in a little pig brain then no one would notice once it was cooked. Pies are checked carefully these days. But they just don't taste as good as they used to, do they? Someone isn't using their brain.

"But you don't, Alice!" Dreep explained.

"Don't I?"

"No! You can go back to the street corner selling matches in the ice and snow. You can sleep in that burnt out house by the shipyards the way you used to. You can scavenge in shop bins for scraps of food like you used to. You don't have to stay here and suffer with Smiff. The door is over there – close it behind you." He spoke softly but his gooseberry-green eyes were as cold as the North Sea.

Alice sat down. "I will stay. But not for simple Smiff. It's like we said before. We are doing this for the Mixly family." Her thin mouth shut like a mousetrap. End of argument.

"Now, where were we?" Dreep asked, smiling again. "Mr Turnip said the driver can stop the engine. So we have one week to train him as an engine driver."

"Me? No one would give a job to me. I'm fresh out of Darlham Gaol and I have the Turnip name," the old man objected.

"No, your name is Urnip and you worked as a coach driver for Lord Fumble. Now that his coaches are idle he wants you to learn how to become an engine driver," Dreep said. Then he added an awful joke.[29]

"He wants you to re-train! Ha! Ha!"

No one laughed (can you blame them?).

"He's right, though," Alice said. "No one will give him a job."

"They will if Lord Fumble orders it," Dreep said. "And I have here a letter from Lord Fumble doing just that!" The teacher placed a sheet of writing paper on the desk and the students bent their heads to read it.

> *The Manager*
> *Wildpool and Helton Railway Company*
> *Wildpool Station*
> *Station Road*
> *Wildpool*
> *16 February 1837*
>
> *Dear Sir*
>
> *This letter is to introduce Richard Urnip to you. The man has served as a coach driver on Lord Fumble's Darlham Estates for forty years. He is the most reliable*

29 . . . one that I am almost ashamed to repeat, it is so bad.

and hard-working person ever to have been in our employ.

However, now the carriage work is reduced. His lordship does not want to dismiss such a loyal servant. He wants Urnip to be taught how to drive a steam locomotive on the Wildpool and Helton Railway. There will be a special train that will run from Fumble Hall to Wishington Country Manor on Monday 27 February 1837. His lordship would be pleased if Urnip could drive the locomotive that day.

Yours faithfully

Andrew Brown – Estate Manager

The class were amazed at the letter. "Where did you get this, Mr Dreep?" Smiff asked.

The teacher shrugged. "I have friends in the Wildpool world of crime. I know my share of forgers and they produced this for me."

"It's perfect," Smiff said.

"It's all right I suppose," Alice grumbled.

Nancy cleared her throat and said softly, "We have a problem. . ."

Chapter 6

FIEVES AND
FIREMEN

Fumble Hall – Thursday 16th February 1837

Lord Jeremiah Fumble, 16th Lord of the Fumble family, sat in the topmost tower of Fumble Hall. Downstairs the floors were marble, the ceilings covered with gold leaf and from the walls hung portraits of all the great Fumbles in history. After forty years as a judge he was losing count of the men, women and children he had sent to foul fates. That was a sadness. He liked to remember every one of the fearful faces, the sobs of shock and the fainting fits that his savage sentences brought on. On winter nights the memories warmed him like glowing coals.

"The Fumbles came across with William the Conqueror," Lord Fumble used to boast. "Sir Giles de Fumble was such a great warrior he was rewarded with these lands at Wildpool."[30]

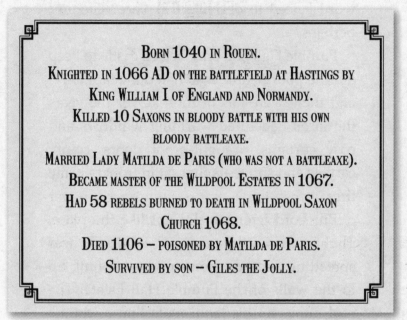

BORN 1040 IN ROUEN.
KNIGHTED IN 1066 AD ON THE BATTLEFIELD AT HASTINGS BY KING WILLIAM I OF ENGLAND AND NORMANDY.
KILLED 10 SAXONS IN BLOODY BATTLE WITH HIS OWN BLOODY BATTLEAXE.
MARRIED LADY MATILDA DE PARIS (WHO WAS NOT A BATTLEAXE).
BECAME MASTER OF THE WILDPOOL ESTATES IN 1067.
HAD 58 REBELS BURNED TO DEATH IN WILDPOOL SAXON CHURCH 1068.
DIED 1106 – POISONED BY MATILDA DE PARIS.
SURVIVED BY SON – GILES THE JOLLY.

Visitors to Fumble Hall were shown around the gloomy pictures of gloomy, glaring men with horses, and gloomy men without horses.

30 The lands at Wildpool were owned by the Saxons. William the Conqueror could not "give" the lands to anyone. The Normans just "stole" the land and battered anyone who tried to argue. The Fumble family were fieves ... sorry, thieves. In 1837 the last Lord Fumble was the biggest thief of them all.

There were some gloomy pictures of horses without gloomy men ... but even the horses looked gloomy. No wonder Lord Fumble wanted to escape Fumble Hall. What is the word I need to describe the place? Gloomy, perhaps?

Fumble Hall had once been a castle to keep out the poor people who hated the family ... and there were lots of those. Over the years the lords had fitted warming windows and cosy curtains, draught-proof doors, comfy carpets and soft seats that sat in front of coaly fires.

But Lord Jeremiah did not like the place. The scruffy little town of Wildpool was spreading and new houses were pushing up to the walls of the Fumble Hall Estate. The coal mines on his land made him a fortune but they were filthy and fouled the air with smoke and choking dust.

"I want a new house in the country," he had told his estate manager, Andrew Brown, three years ago. "Near enough to my mines and my money ... but away from these *common* people. Wishington Country Manor is old – I want to knock it down and build a fine new Wishington Country Manor. But I need money. A million pounds should do it."

Brown spread his hands. "The railway is the coming thing, my lord," Brown said. "That's the way to make a million." He was a grey and grinning ghoul of a man. His hands twisted around one another like slippery snakes.

"Can I afford to build a railway? I don't want to risk my money. It's taken me years to squeeze my million pounds from the peasants in the fields and the miners in the mines. Do you realize ninety of the foolish men died last year when Helton South exploded? Have you any idea how much that cost?"

"Ninety lives, perhaps?" Brown said in his slithery voice.

"It cost me thousands of pounds. We had no coal for a week while they dug out the corpses. Why, I even paid the widows of the dead men. I gave them the wages their husbands would have earned in a week. A whole week!"

"And then threw them out of their cottages, my lord, to bring in new miners," Brown reminded him.

"Brown!" Lord Fumble fumed. "I did not throw them out. They are my cottages. Since their men no longer worked in *my* mines I asked them to find somewhere else to live."

"And if they had nowhere?"

His lordship stabbed a fat finger at his manager. "There are workhouses, Brown. Workhouses for the poor who are too idle to work."

"Yes, my lord," Brown bowed and writhed. "Some are too old or sick to work," he said quietly. "They need your help." Lord Fumble paced the room and ignored his pitiful plea.

"So how do I build a railway? I don't want to risk the Fumble fortune!"

"Sell 'shares', my lord. Sell a thousand shares at a thousand pounds a time and you will have a million pounds. A railway will serve your mines and cost just a hundred thousand pounds or so. Promise the share-holders that it will link up with the main lines and, when the railway is making money, they will make a fortune ... a hundred pounds a year at least. They can live on the hundred pounds a year ... or they can sell their share for two thousand pounds!"

"Are there enough stupid and greedy people to fall for that?"

"Oh, yes, my lord. The world is full of stupid and greedy people ..." then he pulled out a handkerchief to wipe his wet lips and muttered, "You only have to look into a mirror to see one."[31]

That had been three years ago. Now the new Wishington Country Manor had been built and it was time to move.

As I said, Lord Jeremiah Fumble, 16th Lord of the Fumble family, sat in the topmost tower of old Fumble Hall. It was not a fine room but it was the safest place to store gold. There was only one stairway up to the top room and three doors, each opened with different keys.

31 And, let's face it, Andrew Brown could have looked in the mirror and seen a greedy man. Make no mistake, some of Lord Fumble's million found its way into the Brown pockets. When it comes to money you can't trust anyone.

The gold glowed in the light of a lantern. It was polished gold, worn smooth by Fumble fingers. Each coin was loved by the lord. Each coin was placed in one of two oak chests that were bound with iron bands and locked with unbreakable locks.

"I'll see you again when we get to our new home in Wishington Country Manor. Farewell, my lovelies!"

Master Crook's Crime Academy – Thursday 16th February 1837

In the classroom of Master Crook's Crime Academy, quiet Nancy had shocked the class by speaking out so boldly. "We have a problem," Nancy had said.

"I learn to make a locomotive go," Rick Turnip said. "I learn to make it stop. No problem."

"You aren't alone on the footplate," Nancy said. "There is a fireman there with you. The man that keeps the fires going. All sorts of things could go wrong."

"Go on," Samuel Dreep urged her.

"The fireman could try to stop you and you could get hurt. The fireman could share the blame and be hanged ... even though it wasn't his fault. The fireman may have to flee for his life and leave his wife and children to the workhouse."

"So what's the answer, Nancy?" Alice asked.

"We need a fireman on the footplate as well as Mr Turnip as the driver. Someone from the school."

Smiff jumped to his feet. "I can do that!"

Dreep stroked his chin with his long fingers. "Put some coal on the fire, Smiff, while I think this through," he said.

Smiff walked across to the fireplace, took a shovel and pushed it into the coal. "No!" the teacher cried. "Pick up the whole bucket and throw some coal on to the fire."

Smiff shrugged. He reached out for the handle of the large coal scuttle. He tugged. It barely moved from the hearth. He heaved, it rose about the thickness of a toad's toe and then he had to drop it. He tumbled backwards.

Nancy rose and crossed to him. "Let me

help," she said. She picked up the bucket easily and scattered coal on the fire.

"I think we have found our fireman," Dreep said.

"But. . ." Smiff began to object.

"Nancy has been carrying coal buckets up and down stairs at the mayor's house for years. She's the strongest person in the room."

"Yeah . . . but a fireman can't be a firewoman!" Smiff grumbled.

"We'll cut her hair and send her with Mr Turnip as a boy . . . his grandson, shall we?"

Smiff blew out his cheeks. He was fed up, but saw the sense.

And so it was agreed.

The plan took a long time to make but at last Dreep had it written down.

The great Wildpool Train Robbery

MONDAY 20TH FEB

- Rick Turnip and Nancy present themselves at Wildpool Engine Works as trainee driver and fireman. (Nancy will have had her hair cut by the way.)

TUESDAY 21ST FEB

2:00 p.m. Smiff and Samuel Dreep will take a hay wagon from the Crime Academy and drive it to the spot where the Great North Road crosses the Wildpool line to Wishington Country Manor.
(This will be a test run for Monday.)

WEDNESDAY 22ND FEB

8:00 a.m. Rick Turnip and Nancy start work on the Helton Colliery coal train.

SUNDAY 26TH FEB

Day off. Some students may wish to go to church. Some (no names mentioned, Alice) may need to go more than others.

MONDAY 27TH FEB

8:00 a.m. Rick Turnip and Nancy drive the Helton Colliery coal train. They take locomotive No. 2.
2:00 p.m. Smiff and Samuel Dreep will take a hay wagon from the Crime Academy and drive it to the spot where the Great North Road crosses the Wildpool line to Wishington Country Manor. (Allow 1 hour and 30 minutes for journey. We will check the timing later.)
3:00 p.m. Locomotive No. 2 travels to Fumble Hall where a carriage full of gold will be waiting.
3:10 p.m. Nancy will pretend to check the couplings and will unfasten Lord Fumble's carriage and the Guard's Van

with the police officers on board.
3:15 p.m. Locomotive **No. 2** will travel west out of
Fumble Hall. It will be driven to the spot where the Great
North Road crosses the Wildpool line to Wishington
Country Manor. (Allow 30 minutes for journey.)
3:45 p.m. Locomotive **No. 2** will arrive at the crossing
with the Great North Road. Gold transferred to wagon
and hidden under hay. Rick Turnip and Nancy abandon
train. All return to Crime Academy.

TUESDAY 28TH FEB
6:00 p.m. Meeting of shareholders of Helton and
Wildpool Railway. £1,000,000 given back to shareholders.
**7:00 p.m. BIG CRIME ACADEMY PARTY. ANOTHER
JOB WELL DONE.**

Mister Dreep pinned the plan on the
classroom noticeboard.

"Perfect," he said. "Nothing can go wrong.
Nothing."[32]

---

32 Oh, dear. Oh, dear. Oh-dear-oh-dear-oh-DEAR. What happens
when someone says that?

Darlham Gaol – Thursday 16th February 1837

In Darlham Gaol a boy was led in through the great green gates. The prison officer took the chains off his wrists and off his legs.

The governor of the prison stepped out of his office to meet the newcomer.

The little boy's lip trembled like a swallow's wing and tears flowed down his dirty cheeks.

"Alexander Adams, sir," he said wearily. "Found guilty by Justice Fumble in Wildpool. Sentenced to three months in the gaol for picking a gentleman's pocket and stealing a silk handkerchief."

"Still as harsh as ever after all these years," the governor chuckled. He wrapped an arm around the trembling boy's shoulders. "Been to gaol before, Adams?"

The boy shook his head and tears splashed on the stone paving. "No . . . sir . . . I only . . . only took it to keep Mum out of the workhouse. Dad has all our money tied up in the railway shares."

"I understand," the governor said. "We have a few more like you. So dry your eyes!

We have an old gentleman in here who looks after new lads like you!"

"Do you sir?" the boy asked, drying his eyes.

"Yes! The famous old highwayman, Rick Turnip."

"I've heard of him," the boy gasped. "And he'll look after me?"

"Yea . . . er . . . oh, dear me . . . no! I forgot . . . he's not with us any more! Oh no! What shall I do without him?"

"Never mind you!" the boy wailed. "What am I going to do without him."

His pitiful sobs would have melted a heart of the coldest Darlham Gaol stone.[33]

---

33 A tragic thought, eh? Melting a heart of stone. Except I have never in fact met anyone with a heart made of Darlham Gaol stone. Not even Lord Fumble. His heart was the same squidgy and blood-filled sack that we all have. But never mind. Imagine it.

Chapter 7

BOILERS AND
BAILIFFS

**Wildpool Engine Works – Wednesday 22nd
February 1837**

The driver of Locomotive No. 2 was in
a rage. He was dressed in his green,
corduroy suit and black cap. He was a man
of wire in the body and fire in the brain. His
badge said, "William Rump".

He glared at Rick Turnip and Nancy (who
was now dressed as a boy, you will remember.)[34]

Then he glared at the letter for the third
time. It had the crest of the Fumble estates at
the top and the signature of Andrew Brown at

---

34 You DON 'T remember? Oh, come along. Keep up. She has to
pretend she is a boy to get a job as a fireman on the railway. Picture
her with her hair cropped and a coarse, woollen suit on.

the bottom. It ordered the railway company to give Richard Urnip a job AND give him the task of driving the treasure train.

"Do you know what it takes to become an engine driver?"

"Well . . . I've driven coaches for thirty years. . ."

"Aha!" the driver screeched like one of his rusty truck wheels. "It says here forty years!"

"Does it?" Turnip muttered miserably.

Nancy put in quickly, "But you were a footman on the coach for ten years before that . . . that's what Mr Brown should have said."

William Rump the driver turned purple with rage. His eyes bulged as they strained to burst out of his head. "Exactly! Ex-ACT-ly! You have to spend years . . . years . . . before you have the right to be a driver. Years. You start as a cleaner. Getting up before daybreak and crawling under the engine and over the engine and inside the cab, scouring and cleaning and greasing and brushing till you are blacker than the coal in that tender."

Rump jerked his thumb at the tender full of coal behind him.

"But this is urgent," Nancy said softly.

The driver ignored her and raged on, "Then you become a 'Passed Cleaner' – that means you can light the fire in the firebox so it's up to steam when we start . . . that takes about ten years and THEN you can become a fireman. And after ten years as a fireman you can become a driver and after ten years as a driver . . ."

"You'll probably be too old to see where you're going," Rick Turnip muttered.

". . . you become a main line driver."

"On the Helton and Wildpool railway? You can only go ten miles in any direction . . . it's not what you'd call main line, is it?" the highwayman argued.

"So, you want to get thirty years' work into three days? Is that right?" Driver Rump sneered.

"It's an emergency," Nancy said with a quiet smile. "There are only two drivers for the two Wildpool and Helton locomotives . . .

and you have to have a day off, don't you? I mean. You work harder than anyone I've ever met," she added. "You deserve a day off."

The driver sniffed. "I do. But his lordship could bring in proper drivers from other railway companies," he grumbled.

Turnip shook his old head slowly. "They wouldn't come. He pays the meanest wages in the railway world."

Rump nodded, glum.

"And," Nancy added, "he buys the cheapest steam locomotives. They are so badly made they are dangerous."

Rump suddenly lost the wire in his body and his head fell forward. "Locomotive No. 1 exploded," he nodded. "The driver, Johnny, was like a brother to me. And the fireman was a lad with a wife and two children. Terrible."

"They buried them in Wildpool," Nancy said, holding the driver's trembling arm. "I remember there was a big funeral in the town. The mayor gave a speech. I heard him practising."

"You did?"

"I was his maid," Nancy said then snapped her mouth shut and wished she could snap back the words.

"His what?"

"Ahem. . ." she choked. "I . . . I was his . . . maid's . . . brother! No! I mean I am his maid's brother," she managed to say.

The driver nodded. "It was a good speech," he said. "I remember Mayor Twistle's speech. He said the drivers were the heroes of the modern age . . . explorers at the frontiers of the world."

Nancy said, "Mayor Twistle said the driver and the fireman did not die in vain!"

"No. They died in bits," the driver sighed. "In fact . . . between you and me . . . there were not a lot of bits in those coffins. They were scattered a fair way round Wildpool and Helton. What they didn't find I guess the dogs and the foxes must have eaten by now."

Nancy felt a little sick at the thought.[35]

Driver Rump gave another deep sigh then

---

35 I hope you don't. It 's not as if someone asked you to pick up the pieces. Now THAT would make most people sick. But in all the horrific railway accidents someone has to do it. I wonder who?

turned to the Crime Academy pair. "Sorry . . . you're right. We need all the help we can get. If I'm bitter about Lord Fumble and his mean ways, I shouldn't take it out on you two, should I?"

"I understand," Nancy said.

The driver rubbed his hands together. "Then let's get started. You, lad . . . what's your name?"

"Nan— Norman," Nancy said.

"Right, Norman. The driver may turn the knobs and push the levers and turn the wheels . . ."

"And get the most shillings," Nancy said.

"That as well . . . but it is the fireman that makes the fire that heats the water that makes the steam. Not only is it a hot and sweaty job but it is also the one that needs the most skill. You don't just throw coal into the firebox!"

"No?"

"Oh, no! You have to scatter it in just the right way and in just the right amount. Too much and you make black smoke and sparks. Too little and the ash falls through the grate. Too hot and the steam just blows away through the valves – too cool and your locomotive can't pull the bonnet off a baby."

"I've spent five years keeping the mayor's fire going. . ." Nancy began, then remembered to keep her lips sealed.

For the next hour she learned all about firebars and smoke tubes, brick arches and firebeds, the difference between Bedwas coal and Durham coal and how to check if the fire is burning just right.[36]

The fire was built up till it was perfect and Driver Rump turned to the controls. "I move this lever to make the train go faster or slower," he said.

Nancy turned to Rick Turnip. "That's the regulator," she said.

"How do you know that?" Rump exclaimed.

"I read some books about steam locomotives before we came here," she said. "Was that all right?"

---

36 The fireman has to see that the smoke is light grey . . . not too dark and not too light, but just right. A bit like Goldilocks and her porridge . . . except you don't see the Three Bears driving a train.

Rump blinked. "Very admirable, young man. Very. I like the cut of your jib."[37]

By the end of the day they had made two trips to Helton Colliery and carried two loads down to the coal drops at the river edge.

By the time the two Crime Academy companions reached home that evening it was dark and it took them two baths each to get clean.

"Well?" Samuel Dreep asked as they walked through the door of Master Crook's Crime Academy.

"So much to learn," Rick Turnip sighed.

Nancy smiled. "But Mr Turnip is so clever we'll be ready to drive solo by the end of the week. Don't worry. He's a genius."

The old man blushed. "I've been called a few things in my time . . . but never a genius," he chuckled and settled into a chair.

Wildpool Town – Thursday 23rd February 1837

There was a knock at the door while Mrs Mixly was feeding her children cabbage soup

---

37 This is something sailors usually say. But of course the railways had only been running a dozen years or so in 1837. Who knows what Driver Rump had done before he joined the railway company? A mole catcher perhaps?

for dinner. She had picked up the leaves from the market cobbles when the stalls had shut down for the night. The two gold coins were kept to buy food for their father.

"Who's that at the door?" she asked.

Millie and Martin looked at one another. "I hope it's not a thief!" Martin cried and wrapped his arms around the cabbage soup to save it from a soup-snatcher.

Millie spooned her warm, green water quickly into her mouth till it dribbled down her chin.

Mrs Mixly opened the door a crack and saw two young men there. They were tall and almost as wide as the door. Their muscles had muscles and their clothes were as black as the Helton coal. They wore shining top hats and smiles as cunning as cats.

"Mrs Mixly?" the first one asked. "I'm Candy."

"Then my children would love to eat you!" she giggled.[38]

38 Mrs Mixly didn't giggle because she thought her joke was funny. She giggled because she saw two handsome young men and she "came over all silly", as they say. Who says "came over all silly"? Well, I do for a start.

"And I'm Knuckle," the second one said.

"That's handy," the woman said and this time she giggled like a hen because she was sure that was the funniest thing anyone had ever said.

Knuckle blew out his lips in a bored way. "I've never heard that one before."

"Really?" Mrs Mixly smiled. "Not everyone's as witty as me . . . or as pretty as me," she added, trying to flirt.

Candy didn't flirt. "We have been sent by the Northern Brick Bank," he said.

"Oh! They loaned us the money to buy this house!" the woman cried. "How odd that you should call. How lovely to meet you. Come in and take a chair."

"We've come to take them all," Knuckle said. An empty cart stood outside, waiting.

"I don't understand," Mrs Mixly said and her flirty smile was fading as Candy pushed his powerful shoulder against the door and barged into the hall. Mrs Mixly backed into the living room and sat down heavily at her seat at the table.

"Your husband is Maximus Mixly," Knuckle said and he ground the knuckle of his hand into the palm of the other hand.

"Sorry," the woman fluttered. "He's still at work. He works extra hours to make the money to pay for the railway share. Look, there it is above the mantelpiece!" she said proudly.

The two men didn't look. "The thing is, Mrs Mixly, you borrowed money and the bank wants it back. You owe a hundred pounds."

"And the bank shall have it back as soon as the railway starts to pay its way and we are rich," she said.

Candy leaned forward till his beery breath was in her face. "The thing is, Mrs Mixly, the bank can't wait for ever. It wants its money now."

"But we don't have it," she shrugged.

"Then we will take every stick of furniture and sell it and give the money to the bank. We will take every pot and kitchen pan," Knuckle said.

"Every stitch of clothing, boots and shoes and pictures from the walls," Candy added.

"We will sell them and give the money to the bank," he explained.

"And then, if that's not enough, and if you haven't paid the money by the end of the month the bank will take your house," Knuckle chuckled.[39]

"Where will they take our house to?" Millie asked.

Knuckle pulled a pained face. "I mean we will sell your house to someone who can afford to pay."

Martin stood up and looked the bully straight in the belt buckle . . .[40]

"If you take our chairs where will we sit?" the boy asked boldly.

"On the floor," Candy answered.

"If you take our beds then where will we sleep?" Mille asked.

"On the floor."

"And if you sell our house, where would we go?" Mrs Mixly gasped.

39 To have a bully chuckle at your misery is a terrible thing. But, worst of all, is a Knuckle chuckle.

40 Aha! You are waiting for me to say it was a "Knuckle buckle" aren't you? Well, I'm not going to. That would be a pitiful joke and I do not do pitiful.

"Out the door. Not our problem, lady," Candy said. "We are bailiffs. We are only doing our job."

"Throwing a woman and her helpless children out into the cold, cold snow?" Mrs Mixly wailed.

Candy looked at Knuckle. "It's not snowing, is it, Knuckle?"

"Not when we came in," his partner replied. "But don't worry about that now, Mrs Mixly. You have a week to find the money." Knuckle leaned closer to her and hissed, "There is a very good trade in skinny children to sell to chimney sweeps. We could get twenty pounds each for your brats! For now we'll just take the furniture." He lifted the chair, with the woman sitting on it, and carried it as if it was as light as a wren's feather . . .[41]

Mrs Mixley jumped to the floor and fell to her knees. She clung to the leg of the man as he walked to the door. "Please, I beg you on my knees!"

"It's *my* knees you're on," he snarled and kicked her away.

41 and you don't get any feathers lighter than a wren's.

Five minutes later the house was empty. There wasn't even a candle left to warm the little family. All that was left was the railway share in its frame on the mantelpiece. "Please, oh, please don't take that!" Mrs Mixly moaned.

Knuckle looked at Candy and Candy looked at Knuckle. Knuckle looked at the pitiful family sitting in the faint light of the half-moon that shone through the window. "Why would we want to take a Helton and Wildpool Railway share? They are ten a penny – in fact, they aren't even worth the paper they're printed on. The bank would laugh if we took that back with us."

"Only a mug would pay a thousand pounds for that," Candy spat.

"My husband Maximus did," Mrs Mixly sobbed.

"Then he was robbed," Knuckle said. "Robbed."

The men turned and opened the door, letting in the chill wind off the Wildpool river. "Sleep well," they said.

Chapter 8

GUNS AND GETAWAYS

Fumble Hall – Sunday 26th February 1837

The door to Fumble Hall was wide and white. It was meant to look smart and modern but the old building still looked like a crumbling castle . . . with a posh white door instead of a drawbridge. A handle on a rope hung at the side. Police Constable Larch reached up and pulled it.

Deep inside the huge house a bell jangled.

After an age the door was opened by a man dressed as a butler with a black tail coat, grey trousers, white shirt and white cravat tie. "You rang?"

"I am Constable Liddle and this is Constable

Larch. We've come to—"

"Back door!" the butler hissed. "Servants must use the back door."

"I'll have you know we are officers of the law and—" Liddle began but he was speaking to a white door that had been slammed in his face.

"Back door it is," Larch shrugged. His red face was redder than ever and his piggy eyes were more piggy than a pig's. In fact they were so piggy a pig would be ashamed to have eyes like that.

They tramped along the overgrown path, through clumps of cold, damp grass, round the side of the Hall till they reached the green kitchen door.

Larch said, "Leave this to me," and knocked firmly.

The door opened and a man stood there dressed in country clothes – green tweed suit and high riding boots. "Yes?" he asked. "What do you want?"

Larch's mouth moved but no words came out. Just sounds at first. "Splutter . . .

splitter . . . splatter . . . butter . . . but . . ." then, "But . . . you're the butler who answered the front door!"

"So? I can't wait all day to answer doors, you know. Lord Fumble wants his money's worth. I am a butler when the front door bell rings, I am his estate manager when business calls. My name is Andrew Brown. And you are. . ."

"I told you at the front door," Liddle said. He was as thin as a chair leg, with a moustache that was whiter than the front door of Fumble Hall.

"You told the butler," Brown argued. "I am no longer the butler. Do I look like a butler?"

"No, but. . ."

"Then tell me your names and your business," Brown ordered.[42]

"We carry your truncheons like flaming torches of justice. Bring light to the darkness of our savage streets," Larch said proudly.

"Yes, yes, yes . . . flaming truncheons are

42 Aha! you cry. This is the man who was with Lord Fumble just a chapter or two ago. Why is the humble Fumble servant suddenly Brown the bully? Because some people are like that. They crawl to the powerful but boss the less-posh. There is a name for people like that. The name is "creep".

all very well. Nice and warm on a day like today. Just be careful you don't set fire to the curtains. But what I mean is, what are you doing here today?"

"We have come to talk about the guard job we're doing tomorrow," Liddle said.

"Guarding the Fumble Fortune!" Larch said in an awed voice. "Over a million pounds, they say!"

Andrew Brown twisted his pale hands together. "A dangerous job! If any of the Wildpool villains knew about this they would cut your throat as soon as look at you. They would all want to get their hands on this fortune!"

"Cut our throats?" Liddle choked.

"As soon as look at us?" Larch squawked.

"And your flaming truncheons would do you no good at all," Brown added. "What you need are some real weapons!"

"Real weapons?" the policemen chimed together like the front and back door bells.

"And we have them here in Fumble Hall," Brown smiled.

"Suits of armour?" Liddle asked.

"That would keep the knives out," Larch breathed.

"Swords and shields and crossbows and battleaxes . . . a flaming battleaxe would be better than a flaming truncheon, Larch," Liddle said.

"Not sure I could use a sword, a shield, a crossbow and a flaming battleaxe," Larch complained. "I haven't got enough hands."

"I see what you mean. . ." Liddle began.

"No!" Brown cried. "Not the old weapons. I meant the new weapons. Lord Fumble likes to go shooting grouse and pheasants. . ."

"That's against the law!" Liddle gasped. "He can't go round shooting his farm workers! Can he?"

"Pheasants, Liddle, not peasants," Larch explained.

"Lord Fumble has some fine shotguns," Brown went on. "No villain with a knife will come near you if you were each carrying a shotgun." He led the way into the main hall of Fumble Hall, over the cold stone floor, past the glowering pictures of the long-gone Fumbles, past the lances and shields, the heads of dead deer and wild boar, the great iron candle-holders with their dead and shrunken candles. It was gloomy. No wonder Lord Fumble wanted to move out. There were tapestries on some of the walls, faded and grey and torn. They seemed to be showing men murdering animals in hunting scenes from long ago.

Brown pushed a tapestry aside and showed them through the heavy door that stood behind. "Here we are, officers, the Gun Room."

All sorts of guns hung on the walls. There were flintlocks and matchlocks, arquebusses and musketoons, coach guns, calivers and carbines, toradors and tanegashimas, petronels and fowling pieces.

"Most of these are just for show," Andrew Brown explained and pointed to an arquebus.

ARQUEBUS

THE MATCH IS CLAMPED IN A CLIP CALLED THE SERPENTINE. SQUEEZING THE TRIGGER FORCES THE SERPENTINE DOWNWARD, AND BRINGS THE BURNING MATCH IN TOUCH WITH THE PRIMING POWDER RESULTING IN A SPURT OF FIRE FLASHING THROUGH THE TOUCHHOLE AND IGNITING THE MAIN CHARGE INSIDE THE BARREL.

Liddle trembled. "I'm afraid of guns. Well . . . not the guns. I'm afraid to guard a train if Constable Larch has one of those things."

"Quite right," Brown said. "I will fill them with gunpowder so, if you have to fire them, the villains will be scared away. But there will be no shot in them. . . Flash, bang! But nothing comes out of the barrel. Here . . . take this blunderbuss. It looks fearsome enough to scare off any highway robber."

He took down another gun from the wall.

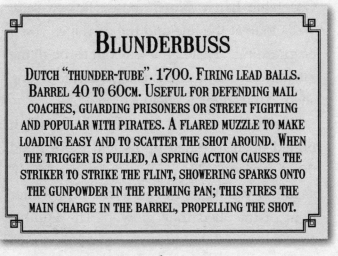

BLUNDERBUSS

DUTCH "THUNDER-TUBE". 1700. FIRING LEAD BALLS. BARREL 40 TO 60CM. USEFUL FOR DEFENDING MAIL COACHES, GUARDING PRISONERS OR STREET FIGHTING AND POPULAR WITH PIRATES. A FLARED MUZZLE TO MAKE LOADING EASY AND TO SCATTER THE SHOT AROUND. WHEN THE TRIGGER IS PULLED, A SPRING ACTION CAUSES THE STRIKER TO STRIKE THE FLINT, SHOWERING SPARKS ONTO THE GUNPOWDER IN THE PRIMING PAN; THIS FIRES THE MAIN CHARGE IN THE BARREL, PROPELLING THE SHOT.

"It scares me," Larch agreed.

Brown smiled. "Many years ago . . . about

forty years I think . . . a highwayman tried to hold up Lord Fumble's coach with a finger hidden under his cloak."

"Where did he get the finger from?" Larch gasped. "Did he cut it off one of his victims?"

Brown shook his head. "Turnip, was the name."

"He cut the finger off a turnip? I didn't know turnips had fingers!"

Brown's mouth twisted madly. "Just take a gun each and get out before I have to shoot Constable Larch. Now," bossy Brown said, "let's look at the line and the carriages you'll be guarding." He led the way out through the kitchen door and across the garden to a long shed at the edge of a field.

A railway line led into the shed. Brown pulled open the shed doors and there stood three carriages. They were painted a bright shade of yellow and even in the dim winter light of the shed they glowed. The Fumble crest decorated the sides.

"First class!" Liddle said. "The poor people have to travel in carriages with no roofs and hard wooden seats. I bet he has satin cushions!"

They climbed aboard the first carriage.

"No satin cushions," Larch said.

"No seat!" Liddle said.

"This is the goods carriage. We'll use this to move all the valuables from Fumble Hall to Wishington Country Manor later on. But tomorrow this will be the carriage we'll use to load the treasure."

The estate manager led the way to the back of the carriage. He opened a door, crossed the link and opened the door into the next carriage. This one smelled of fine leather and rich wine. The yellow silk seats were soft enough to lose a cat in. "Lord Fumble's carriage," Brown said.

"Ohhhh! We'll be very comfortable in here," Liddle said.

Brown sneered, "You won't be IN here . . . you'll be in the guard's van behind."

He led the way into a small brown truck with bare wooden walls and rough wooden shelves that would serve as seats. Liddle and Larch sat carefully on one.

"Comfy enough," Larch said. His seat was padded by his fat bottom.

"Hard as stone," Liddle said. His bony backside felt every splinter of wood on the solid seat.

"It's less than ten miles," Brown said. "Half an hour." He spread out a plan on the small table in the centre of the van.

Liddle and Larch nodded.

"The locomotive will arrive at two p.m. after its second coal run of the day. It will reverse down the branch line to Fumble Hall here and collect these carriages. It will then head west to Wishington Country Manor."

Brown waved a fine, pale finger over the plan. He tapped a spot on the map. "Here is where the railway crosses the Great North Road. If I were a robber then that is where I would stop the train."

"Why?" Liddle asked.

"Because you have to get the gold off the train, on to a wagon and away. You need to stop the train near a road. That, gentlemen, is where we will need you with your guns!"

"Ooooh!" Liddle sighed.

"I think I need a pee!" Larch said as he shivered with the thought of meeting some hideous highwayman.

The train with the empty coal trucks struggled up the hill to Helton. "We haven't enough power, Nancy," Rick Turnip sighed as he pushed the regulator as hard over as he could.

Nancy nodded. "I know. That's the tricky bit about being a fireman. You can't make too much steam or it's wasted. But you can't make too little or we run out . . . like we have now."

The locomotive spluttered and spat and the cranks clattered slower and slo-wer and sl-ooo-www-errr.

"So what's the answer? It's no good running out of steam tomorrow if the police are chasing us!"

"The answer is to learn the line," Nancy explained. "If I know the hills are coming up then I can get just the right amount of steam. When we do this run again this afternoon I'll be better."

"But we're not doing this run tomorrow. Tomorrow we're going to Wishington Country Manor," the old man pointed out.

Nancy nodded. "So, we finish the second run but instead of going back to Wildpool engine shed we tell the railway policeman to turn the points toward Wishington Country Manor!"

"Will he do that?"

"Wave the Fumble family paper under his nose and he will," the girl smiled.

Turnip nodded. "It'll be getting dark by then, but you're right. You know, Nancy, you have a great criminal brain."

"But I'll never be as famous as you," she said and began to sing softly as she shovelled coal and built up the steam again.

"Tommy Turnip is no good
Chop him up for fire wood
If the fire won't burn his head
Use his wooden arm instead."

Rick Turnip was right. By the time they'd

finished their coal run the sun was setting, blood red, behind ragged silver clouds. They pulled away from Wildpool Coal Drops over the river where the coal ships waited.

They reached the line from Wildpool to the west. The railway policeman said, "Not going back to the sheds for the night?"

"No," Nancy sighed. "Lord Fumble wants us to move some furniture from Fumble Hall to the new Wishington Country Manor."

The railway policeman heaved the lever to set them on the track to the Hall. "I hope he's paying you overtime," he said.

"Not a chance," Rick Turnip grumbled.

"You'll be the last train out tonight so I'll leave the points set so you go straight back to the sheds," the railway policeman promised and waved them goodnight.

The locomotive headed west towards the dying light. They passed the Fumble Hall branch; Nancy changed the points so they could back down the line towards the Hall. They arrived in the dark parkland and shuddered to a halt just before their wagons bumped into the shed with the yellow carriages.

"Right," Nancy said. "Let's do a trial run to Wishington Country Manor." She turned over the Fumble letter which was grubby by now and as they moved forward she marked how many minutes there were between the climbs and the falls and how steep they all were.

After half an hour they came to the Great North Road. Turnip gave a long blast of the steam whistle and cows by the roadside ran for their lives.

"How long to unload the gold?" Nancy asked.

"Five minutes," the highwayman said.

"So I have five minutes to build up the steam for a fast getaway," Nancy said and marked the spot on the map.

"No, no!" Turnip cried. "Once we empty the Fumble Fortune at the road here we abandon the train. That's the plan!"

"But if we leave it here then Inspector Beadle's policemen will find it all the quicker."

"They can't run after a train!" the highwayman said with a frown.

"No . . . but if they think quickly they could saddle up one of his lordship's horses. They would catch up soon after we stopped here. If I take the train on to the end of the line they'll follow the train, not your slow wagon. You'll have much more time to get away!"

"But what about you?" the highwayman asked.

"I can jump off as the train runs out of steam near the Country Manor and walk back to the Crime Academy. We'll meet up there."

"I don't like you taking that risk," Turnip moaned.

"I'll be all right," Nancy said. "I'll be fine."[43]

As the sun had set over Fumble Hall there had been a light in the topmost tower room. Lord Fumble had been stroking his precious chests of gold. "I love you so much, my lovelies, I think I will have you buried with me. We can't have you falling into the hands of the poor, can we? They'd only spend you

---

43 Oh, dear. Master Crook is a Master Crook. If he makes a plan you have to stick to it. Start making changes to the plan and you are heading for trouble. I can just see it coming . . . as one cow on the railway line said to the other. But it was the last thing that cow ever said. Know what I mean?

on food. Such a waste that would be."

The shuffling sound of the locomotive made him move to the window and look out over the gardens to the railway shed.

He watched as a line of empty coal trucks shunted down the line to his private platform. The train stopped. Fire flared in the locomotive cab, the fire door closed and the train set off again.

"Curious," Lord Fumble mumbled. "I must remember to mention this to Brown."

Brown was down in the dining room, dressed as a butler and ready to serve dinner. "Nothing to worry about, my lord," he said and began to wring his hands. "The engine crew must be practising. I believe they are new men . . . replacing the ones that were . . . err . . . blown apart."

"That will be it," Lord Fumble nodded.

But as Brown walked to the kitchen he said quietly, "Curious. I must forget to mention this to Inspector Beadle!"

Chapter 9

SECRETS AND A SHOVEL

Monday 27th February 1837

Nancy was a bright girl. She soon learned the skill of being a fireman, and what a skill it is! We all remember 12 June 1899 and Armagh. That date is burned in the memories of railway men and women.

ARMAGH TRAIN TRAGEDY: 80 DEAD, 250 INJURED

LOCOMOTIVE FAILS ON STEEP, 3-MILE CLIMB

Nancy got it right. She sweated and puffed as much as Locomotive No. 2 but still found time to look out of the cab and wave at the trains-potters by the roadside.

Rick Turnip and Nancy drank large mugs of tea at Helton Colliery while they waited for their coal trucks to be filled.

"It's a good life," the old man sighed. "If I hadn't gone to Darlham Gaol I could have been an engine driver." He took out a grubby handkerchief and wiped away a tear or two.

"Are you crying for your wasted years in gaol?" the girl asked.

"No . . . I'm crying cos I miss my old life in the prison cell . . . the library . . . all the friends I made."

Nancy stroked his arm. "You have friends in the Crime Academy. And you're enjoying this, aren't you?"

The highwayman tried to give her a cheerful smile through his soot-stained face. "I suppose so. I did so much good at Darlham though. I helped all the frightened new prisoners settle in."

"You're doing good if you steal the Fumble Fortune," Nancy said. "There are people starving in the streets because that loathsome lord tricked them out of their money." She remembered seeing a cart-load of the Mixlys' furniture as it rolled past the windows of the Crime Academy.

Alice had sighed, "Some other poor soul has lost their furniture. They'll lose their house next and be out on the streets like I was. In winter too."

"They could be moving house," Nancy had tried to argue.

Alice had looked at her with pity. "Not when the cart's being led by Candy and Knuckle. They're the bank bailiffs. That's probably some other poor victim of the Fumble fraud."

Rick Turnip gave a sharp nod. He put down his empty tea mug. "You're right, lass. Let's fill up our water tank and we'll be on our way!"

"One more trip here then we're ready for the first great train robbery! You'll be as famous as Tom Turnip . . . more famous!" she laughed.

At two p.m. Samuel Dreep stepped out of the Crime Academy on to the path that led to the front door.

A cart stood there. The piebald horse was held by two men as wide as Locomotive No. 2.

"Good afternoon, Mr Candy, good afternoon, Mr Knuckle," the teacher said.

"Afternoon," the two men grunted. Smiff stood a little way behind him and glared at them. He knew how these two men made their money.

"Thank you for hiring me your cart," Dreep said and stroked his fine moustache.

"Half a crown, you said," Candy reminded him.

The teacher took some silver from his pocket. "Half a crown each is what it's worth to me," Dreep said. "After all, you could be losing business. You could be out there tearing toys from some child's little hands, or bottles from babies, or washing from women or squeezing money from men or cribbing coins from the blind beggar on the corner of the High Street!"

"You what?"

"I said, you do a wonderful job for the bank. Thanks to brave lads like you the poorhouse is full of families, the banks are crammed with cash and the Fumble Fortune is fatter than you!"

Knuckle nodded. "That's true, sir. Where would the world be without people like us? Where?"

"It has been a pleasure doing business with you, gentlemen," Dreep said smiling, but his grin was grim. "Now, Smiff, time to collect a little hay and then it's off to the Great North Road."[44]

At three p.m., Locomotive No. 2 had dropped its second load of coal and was headed west on the line.

When they reached the branch to Fumble Hall the railway policeman gave Rick Turnip a cheerful wave. "Afternoon, Mr Urnip. Off to the Hall?"

"That's right. Special job. This job is so secret there are only two people in the world who know what we'll be carrying – me and Lord Fumble."

"Ooooh! Yes! You have to be careful! If any villains found out you was carrying the Fumble Fortune they'd be all over you like

---

44 I know, Master Crook could have hired a cart from lots of places. He just liked the idea of using the bank bullies' wagon to carry away the cash. He was a strange man was Master Crook.

wasps round a jam pot!" the man said as he pushed the points lever to send them on the track towards the Hall.

"That's right," Turnip agreed. "Only you, me and Lord Fumble know about the treasure."

"And me," Nancy put in.

"Yes," the highwayman nodded, "only you, me, Norman here and Lord Fumble know about the treasure."

"Exactly what the estate manager Mr Brown said last night!" the railway policeman agreed.

Turnip sighed. "Only you, me, Norman, Mr Brown and Lord Fumble know!"

"That's what I told the lads in the tavern last night!"

"Thank you and good afternoon," the highwayman snapped.

"Right. See you in half an hour," the railway policeman said with a wave.

Turnip backed the locomotive down the branch to the Fumble Hall shed. "It seems so many people know about this trip we'll be lucky if we aren't robbed fifty times before we meet with Mr Dreep. The secret of being a good highwayman is . . . well . . . to know a secret. But, if everyone knows, then it isn't a secret any more! Steady with the steam there, Nancy, we'll probably have to wait a while for them to load the treasure."

Nancy rested on her shovel and looked over the tender towards the carriage shed. "No. Mr Brown is waiting. Those policemen, Liddle and Larch look as if they're loading the treasure coach already."

"All the better. The less time we spend there the better. You know what to do?"

"Yes," Nancy said and her heart was flapping in her chest like a sparrow in a greenhouse trying to get out.

The train slowed to a halt and gently bumped against the treasure carriage. Nancy jumped down, climbed under the tender of Locomotive No. 2 and fastened the coupling to the carriage. She then hurried along the side of the track.

"Where are you going?" Constable Liddle asked. He waved an ugly gun towards her.

"To check that the carriages are all coupled safely," Nancy said. She held up her hands that were black with coal and grease. "I don't mind if you do it!" she offered.

Liddle stepped back. "No! No, lad. You carry on!"

"I thought you might say that," the girl murmured and went to the coupling between the treasure coach and his lordship's travelling carriage. She shook the linking chain. It was tight. These carriages were hardly ever separate. They had been joined for three years and were stuck fast.

Nancy ran to the cab of the locomotive, grabbed her shovel and ran back. She used the shovel to hammer at the link and shake the rust free. Lord Fumble heaved his heavy body out of his carriage. "What's all the noise?"

"Sorry, sir," Nancy said. She looked up at the fat face of the lord and the man stared back at her.

"Don't I know you from somewhere?" he asked.

"No, sir," she said.

"I never forget a face!" he argued and stared harder. "I have seen you before."

"I . . . er . . . used to work for Mayor Twistle," she remembered. "You were sometimes a guest at the house."

"And you?"

"I was . . . a footman!"

"You're a bit small to be a footman," the lord snapped.

"That'll be why you remember her!" Andrew Brown said helpfully.

"No, Brown . . . I remember her from a long time ago . . . thirty or forty years ago." He stroked his chin and climbed back into his carriage to have a glass of port and try to remember.

Nancy's hands were shaking so much she almost missed the link with the next swing of her shovel but it caught and the link fell loose.

"Only Master Crook and Mr Dreep know my secret," she moaned as she lifted the heavy chain off the hook. "I hope we get away before Lord Fumble remembers!"

Alice huddled in her warm woollen coat, gloves and scarf. Since being at Master Crook's Crime Academy she didn't shiver in the whistling winter winds any more. Now Master

Crook made sure she was warm and well fed.

She knocked at the door and the knock sounded hollow – like tapping on an empty box.

The woman who answered the door had two children clinging to her skirts. Their eyes were hollow and hopeless with hunger. "If you've come to take the furniture away you're too late. There isn't any left."

Alice swallowed tears. "No," she said. "No . . . I came to deliver a leaflet." She checked the list Master Crook had given here. "Mrs Mixly?"

"Yes."

"Read this . . ."

> THE SHAREHOLDER
> WILDPOOL AND HELTON RAILWAY COMPANY
> 27 FEBRUARY 1837
>
> DEAR SIR OR MADAM
> THIS LETTER IS TO INFORM YOU THAT LORD FUMBLE WILL
> BE PAYING A DIVIDEND TO ALL SHAREHOLDERS OF THE
> HELTON AND WILDPOOL RAILWAY.
> PLEASE PRESENT YOURSELF TO THE APOLLO MUSIC HALL,
> WILDPOOL, SOLE LESSEE – MR FARLAND   AT 6 P.M. ON
> TUESDAY 28 FEBRUARY 1837.
> IMPORTANT. DO NOT FORGET TO BRING YOUR SHARE
> CERTIFICATE WITH YOU. NO PAYMENT WITHOUT A
> CERTIFICATE.
> YOURS FAITHFULLY,
>
> Andrew Brown – ESTATE MANAGER

"Money?" Mrs Mixly sighed.

"Food?" the Mixly twins cried.

"Yes! Tomorrow night you'll have food!" the woman said, crushing the letter in her excitement. "Oh, your dear father always said Lord Fumble was a great man and he'd repay us one day."

"But what will we eat the food off, Ma?" Millie Mixly asked. "We've no table, no plates, no knives, no forks, no spoons."

"We'll buy some," the woman sobbed. "We'll buy some."

Little Millie coughed weakly and slipped to the bare wooden floor. "Ahhhh!" she said and fainted.

Alice caught the girl. Alice wasn't much taller than the Mixly twin but little Millie was just a cotton dress full of bones. The Crime Academy pupil spoke quickly. "No need to wait for tomorrow to eat, though. We've plenty of food up at my school . . . most of the students are out rob . . . er . . . on a school trip. I've got thick soup and fresh bread, fresh fried fish from the market and creamy custards."

"Ooooh!" Mrs Mixly swooned at the thought.

"No! Don't you go fainting too!" Alice cried. "I can't carry you all up the hill. Come on, follow me. We'll have you fed from your toes to your head in no time."

The Mixlys followed Alice on to the street.

Alice walked quickly and remembered the argument she'd had that lunch time with Master Crook in the dark basement. "How come Smiff and Nancy get the exciting job – robbing a train. And you give ME the boring old job of taking leaflets round the houses. I'm not some blooming serving maid like Nancy, you know."

Master Crook had given a deep sigh. "Alice, we are like pieces on a chessboard – we all have different jobs to do. But we are working to the same end – to defeat Fumble's wicked plan. Smiff and Nancy get the excitement but you, Alice . . . you get the joy of bringing happiness to Fumble's victims."

"Who says? You says?" she'd barked back.

Now, as she opened the door into the Crime

Academy kitchen, and saw the tear-stained faces of the marvelling Mixlys, she mumbled, "Yeah, all right, Master Crook, you was right."

It was 3:15 and the plan was running on time. Nancy ran to the cab of Locomotive No. 2 and began to feed the firebox with just the right amount of coal for the climb out of Fumble Hall fields.

Rick Turnip watched the steam gauge as the needle swung higher. He had to get away on full power and as quickly as possible. When the gauge was past the mark, the fire roaring, the steam screaming to escape and the boiler bubbling he reached for the regulator.

In the guard's van at the back Constable Liddle suddenly said, "I think one of us ought to sit with the treasure, just in case something goes wrong! Inspector Beadle told us not to let it out of our sight."

Larch argued, "No. He told us not to let that treasure carriage out of our sight. Nothing will go wrong! The estate manager has it all planned. We are just here for the ride. I've never ridden a steam train before. I'm going to enjoy it. I've got a bottle of beer and a cheese sandwich. You go if you want but I'm staying here!"[45]

The tall, thin constable stepped from the guard's van and walked towards the front of the train. He walked past Lord Fumble's carriage and reached the treasure carriage.

At that moment Rick Turnip pushed the regulator. Locomotive No. 2 jumped forward like a stone from a catapult.

There was a crash as the coupling to the treasure carriage went tight. "Here! Don't go without me!" Constable Liddle cried . . . though no one could hear him in the clattering roar of the moving engine. He struggled to pull the door open but it was too stiff. He looked back to see if he could climb aboard Lord Fumble's coach and saw it wasn't moving.

Constable Liddle wasn't as bright as one of his buttons but even he saw what was happening. "Stop that train!" he cried. As the back of the treasure coach rattled past

45 When he said "I'm staying here," he meant he was staying in the guard 's van. He didn't mean "I'm staying here . . . in the guard 's van at Fumble Hall carriage shed." But we know that 's EXACTLY where he would be.

him he grabbed at one of the flag ropes that was fastened to the back of the yellow coach. He dropped the gun. It struck the iron rail and exploded. It had no bullets in but it did have a cloth backed in to keep the powder in. The burning cloth struck the seat of Liddle's trousers and the wind whipped it into a flame.

His arms ached as he was lifted off his feet. His shining boots sparked and skidded off the platform and he was towed along like a smoking kite on a steam-driven string. "Ooooh! Me bum's on fire!" he wailed but there was no one to hear him.

"We've done it," Nancy cried. "We've escaped with the loot!"[46]

If this was the first great train robbery, then Constable Liddle was the first policeman in the flying squad! His skinny legs flew out behind him like twigs . . . so he was also the first policeman in Special Branch. . .[47]

46 But, oh, Nancy, what's that burning blue thing with silver buttons flapping behind?

47 Twigs . . . Special Branch, geddit? Oh, never mind.

Chapter 10

DARK AND PARK

Nancy worked steadily and had the fire glowing perfectly. Locomotive No. 2 climbed away from Fumble Hall steadily, happy to have a coach with treasure rather than a long line of heavy coal trucks.

They reached the main line in ten minutes and slowed to a halt. Without a guard's van it was tricky because the guard's van had the brakes.[48]

Rick Turnip managed to stop the train

---

[48] Yes, I know that to us modern folk of 1901 a train without brakes is a shocking thing. But true! Drivers just turned off the regulator and let the locomotive drift to a halt. If they wanted a really quick stop they would throw the reverse lever. Dangerous and deadly . . . but so is cholera.

just short of the points where the railway policeman waited.

No one heard the soft thud from the back. As the train stopped moving Constable Liddle stopped flying. He swung forward and smacked into the back of the treasure coach. He fell senseless on to the track. He landed on his backside and at least that smothered the fire in his pants.

"Let us through to the main line," Turnip called.

"Can't do that," the railway policeman said. "The last coal train of the day is on the line, coming the other way. You'll have to wait till it's passed."

"How long?" Nancy asked, anxious. She looked back towards Fumble Hall. No one was coming ... yet. But a fast horse could catch them in ten minutes.

"Ten minutes," the railway policeman said.

Nancy groaned and went about keeping the fire in the box an even glow. She had plenty of coal but it was a while since they'd taken on water. If the boiler ran dry then it could explode ... just as Locomotive No. 1 had done.

Rick Turnip tapped his hands on the regulator. Nancy chewed her nails and that left her with black lips. Lord Fumble and the policemen had been left behind but if there were horses in Fumble Hall stables they could catch them if they waited much longer.

After twelve minutes the coal train from Helton huffed past. The driver of Locomotive No. 3, Driver Rump, gave Turnip a cheery wave. Then the coal-train driver looked ahead and gave a scream.

A figure in a navy uniform and a battered top hat was staggering towards the track in front of him. He threw the engine into reverse and it slowed but not quickly enough. Constable Liddle walked into the side of the cab and bounced back on to the cold ground beside the track.

Nancy watched the coal train in horror and saw the dazed policeman fall. He fell face down and she could see Liddle's scorched buttocks smiling up at the sky. At least the coal train had cleared the points. She cried to the railway policeman, "Let us through . . . in the name of Lord Fumble . . . let us through!"

The man threw the points, Turnip pushed the regulator and Locomotive No. 2 jumped forward on to the main line and headed towards Wishington Country Manor.

Driver Rump on Locomotive No. 3 climbed down and knelt beside the battered Constable Liddle. "What are you doing? Trying to kill yourself?"

Liddle shook his head. "Stop! Thief!" he croaked.

Rump pulled the stopper from his water flask and poured some into Liddle's bleeding mouth which had stained his wisp of white moustache red. The thin policeman struggled to his matchstick legs. "We carry our truncheons like flaming torches of justice. Bring light to the darkness of your savage streets," he croaked. "Follow that train!"

"What train?"

"The train with the Fumble Fortune, of course!"

Rump understood. "Are you saying it's been stolen? But that old man Urnip seemed such a nice old bloke."

"He won't get away from the flaming truncheons of Wildpool police. We always get our man. Inspector Beadle expects every man to do his duty!"

Driver Rump climbed back into his cab and pulled the wild-eyed, white-whiskered Constable Liddle after him.

The picture in the Wildpool Bugle newspaper showed the problem . . .[49]

"I'll have to run backwards," Driver Rump explained. "And we have a heavy load of coal trucks to push ahead of us."

That's when a very unfortunate accident happened. There is not a lot of room on the footplate of a locomotive, and with Rump and his fireman and Constable Liddle it was pretty crowded. Liddle, excited and still a little dazed, drew his truncheon crying, "In the name of the flaming truncheons follow that train!"

49 though you have already worked it out. The coal train was facing the wrong way. . .

As he swung the truncheon like a sword he caught the fireman neatly on the jaw and sent him spinning out of the cab and on to the side of the track. "Now look what you've done!" Rump roared.

"Never mind that . . . follow that train!"

"I can't drive this without a fireman," the driver groaned.

"I will be your fireman . . . your truncheons-of-fire-man in fact! Can you smell burning cloth?"

Rump shrugged and called to the railway policeman to change the points to allow him to reverse towards Wishington Country Manor and to take care of the knocked-out fireman.

By the time he was ready to leave he found Liddle shovelling coal into the firebox. "No, no, no!" he cried. "We have enough steam already . . . you're damping down the fire." Sure enough the chimney of Locomotive No. 3 was pouring out sooty and sparking black smoke.

Rump waved to the guard at the far end of his train to release the brake and they began to roll down the hill. The weight of the coal trucks dragged them along but the choked engine was running out of steam. It was s-l-o-w.[50]

Smiff and Samuel Dreep shivered as they sat at the crossing and waited. The sun was setting behind clouds as grey as slate. And the faces of the Crime Academy crew were grey too. The train was ten minutes late. They wore caps pulled down and scarves covered the bottom halves of their faces. It wasn't just the cold that made them wrap up their faces.

A man sat on a wooden stool by the side of the track and grinned the grin of a simpleton. He wasn't a simpleton – he was a trains-potter, but sometimes it's hard to tell them apart. "Afternoon," he said with a simpleton smile. "Are you trains-potting?"

"Er . . . yes," Smiff said.

"Always happy to meet another trains-potter. My name is Tarquin."

"Pleased to meet you, Tarquin," Smiff mumbled.

---

50 Of course we know that the robbers were heading to a dead-end. No matter how long it took, Liddle and Rump would catch up to Locomotive No. 2 in the end.

"Of course you don't usually see trains on this line," Tarquin the potter explained. "But there's a secret train due any time. I'm the only one that knows about it ... well. Me and the Wildpool East Train Society ... we call ourselves WETS."

"Good name," Smiff muttered into the scarf.

"Of course I had to take an afternoon off work to see this great occasion ... the first train to run to Wishington Country Manor. I will report back to the WETS."

"Report what?" Dreep asked as he huddled inside his long coat.

"Report the number of the locomotive. Since Locomotive No. 1 exploded there are just Locomotive No. 2 and Locomotive No. 3 left. My guess is it will be Locomotive No. 2 or Locomotive No. 3. What do you reckon?"

"I reckon," Smiff said carefully, "that if that train don't get here soon I'm going to have to kill you before you bore me to death."

"Ha! Ha!" the simpleton ... sorry, trains-potter ... laughed. "Just as well I can see it coming then! Showing a clean, light grey smoke . . . sign of a good fireman that."

"Twelve minutes late," Dreep said. "I hope there haven't been problems."

Smiff and Dreep jumped quickly to the road, their freezing feet forgotten, and watched as the smoke trail turned into a locomotive and then they could see the treasure coach glowing yellow in the dying light of the day.

The track ran downhill to the spot where the Crime Academy cart waited at the crossing. Turnip had no brakes so the train was running too quickly and dashed past the waiting robbers.

Old Turnip threw the locomotive into reverse. The whole train clanked and shuddered and complained but it rolled back towards Dreep and Smiff. Still it was another four minutes wasted. They were sixteen minutes behind the planned time.

Dreep and Turnip tugged at the door to the treasure coach as Smiff backed the horse towards the line.

"Locomotive No. 2!" the trains-potter

cried. "Wonderful! I have it in my book. The other WETS will be so-o jealous."

Each treasure chest was heavy but between them – the teacher, the highwayman and the pupils were able to load them both on to the cart.

"Now that is interesting . . . exciting even," Tarquin cried.

"What? We're not doing anything wrong. It's a delivery to a farm," Dreep said as he sweated over a chest full of gold.

"No, no, no!" the simpleton smiled. "I mean it is exciting to see two locomotives on the line at the same time."

"What are you on about?" Smiff grunted.

The trains-potter pointed with his pencil. "There's another locomotive heading this way. Thick, black smoke . . . poor firebox work is that. It'll be slow and it'll probably start fires by the side of the track! Careless. I wonder what number this one is?"

Smiff was sweating and nervous. "I don't suppose it could be Locomotive No. 1, could it?"

"I doubt it . . . unless it's a ghost train."

"Then it's bleeding Locomotive No. 3 then, isn't it?" Smiff exploded.

"I think you may be right," the simpleton said . . . simply.

"The real question is . . . what's it bleeding doing here?" Smiff cried as the second chest of gold was lowered on to the cart and Rick Turnip began to cover both the chests with hay.

"No. The real question is, will it be able to stop in time before it hits this train. I mean, the driver has a guard's van and a row of coal trucks blocking his view. The coal trucks are heavy and the brake on the guard's van won't be strong enough to stop it in time . . . he's running backwards."

"So he throws it into forwards," Rick Turnip said. His eyes were fixed on the coal train that was just half a mile away now.

"Ah! No!" the trains-potter said, wagging his pencil. "That smoking fire won't be heating the boiler . . . there won't be enough steam to send the train forward. No. It looks like a disaster to me. Half a mile at thirty miles per hour – Ooooh! They'll smash into your train in two minutes. Anyone standing here will be killed on the spot! They won't know what hit them. Unless it's me, of course, I would know what hit me because I have been watching. But any passing stranger will be wiped out with flying wood, shredded by shards of metal or sizzled with streams of steam. . ."

But Samuel Dreep had stopped listening. "Climb aboard the cart, Mr Turnip!" he called and reached down a hand to help the old man aboard.

"Nancy!" Smiff called. "Hurry!"

"No, you get away," the brave girl cried. "Your cart is heavy. They can stop, jump off and walk after you. They'll soon catch you. They need to keep following the train."

"The trains-potter says it'll smash into you in two minutes!" Dreep moaned.

"A minute and a half now!" the young man said cheerfully.

"Not if I set away now!" Nancy cried. She threw the regulator to the right the way she'd seen Rick Turnip do and the train wheels skidded and screeched on the iron rails. At last they found some grip and Locomotive No. 2 lurched forward.

"One minute," the trains-potter cried.

Smiff jumped off the cart and grabbed the horse's head-collar and led it down the road back to Wildpool. "Come on, you nag! You'll be dog-food ... steam-cooked dog-food at that. . . Come on!"

The horse plodded slowly. Then Nancy yanked the rope that blew the whistle and the blast startled the horse into a fast trot. As it jogged past Smiff, Dreep reached down and pulled him on to the front seat of the cart. In moments they were safely clear and heading home down the darkening road.

Dreep looked back, horrified as he saw the coal train rumbling down towards the treasure train just as the trains-potter had said it would.

Nancy heaved at the regulator but the whistle blast had cost her a lot of steam.

On the coal train the clumsy coal clutter in the firebox began to burn through and make some steam again. Driver Rump threw the engine into forward.

"Thirty seconds!" the trains-potter clapped. "I can draw an on-the-spot picture for the WETS weekly magazine. I'll be famous! An eye witness!" He turned to a clean page on his number-collecting book and waited. "Twenty seconds," he gasped. He started drawing.

Nancy shovelled coal into the firebox of No. 2 and it began to pull away up the four-mile climb towards Wishington Country Manor.

"Ten seconds!"

The coal train slowed. Its wheels were whirring like an express train and the guard was heaving on the brake lever as if his life depended on it.[51]

Slithering on the evening-damp of the rails the coal wagons rocked, they slowed, they skidded by the trains-potter. "One second and. . ." And Locomotive No. 2 picked up just enough speed to pull away with its empty treasure coach.

51 Maybe that 's because his life did depend on it! The guard's van would be the first to smash into the treasure coach and the guard would be crushed like a spider under a steam hammer, a moth under a mallet or a butterfly under a bum.

The coal wagons crept past the man with the notebook. "We're looking for the Fumble Fortune!" Constable Liddle cried.

"They went that way!" the trains-potter shouted, pointing after Nancy's train.

"Didn't they unload the treasure here?" Rump asked. "We saw the train stop."

"No. They just dropped off farm supplies."

"Then the Fumble Fortune must still be on that train. They can't escape. Follow them!" Liddle said.

Rump shrugged. He signed for the guard to release the brake then used his precious steam to push his load up the hill, westwards towards Wishington Country Manor.

Nancy was half a mile ahead. She could jump off the train at the end of the line and be lost in the darkness of the park around the Country Manor before Constable Liddle arrived. He would need a truncheon of fire to search and he didn't really have one.

So Nancy should have been safe.

She *should* have been safe.

But. . .

Chapter 11

CURTAINS AND CASH

4:00 p.m. Monday 27th February 1837

Nancy made a wonderful fireman. She loved coal. She understood coal. She knew how it burned and could turn the rooms of Mayor Twistle's home toasty in minutes.

She could keep the water in Locomotive No. 2 bubbling as fast or as slow as Rick Turnip wanted.

But you know all that.

So why was Nancy heading for disaster when she was such a wonderful fireman?[52]

She had watched the old highwayman pushing the levers and changing the speed.

52 I will tell you. Nancy was a fireman. She was not an engine driver.

But she had never done it herself . . . until now.

And now she had no one to help. No one to tell her what the levers and handles did, no one to tell her what the dials and pointers meant.

And it was dark. She could only guess how far she was from the buffers at the end of the line. The line that led into the park of Wishington Country Manor.

Nancy let the fire go down and peered ahead. A half-moon glinted on the tracks but that didn't help much. She shut off the regulator and let the engine coast along. But it was running light with only a tender and an empty treasure coach to drag it back.

She saw the creamy stone building of Wishington Country Manor looming ahead. Servants had already lit candles in some of the rooms as they waited for Lord Fumble to arrive.

The end of the line must be very near, she knew, but the engine wasn't slowing enough. She needed to throw the wheels into reverse but she wasn't sure how.

She looked over the side of the cab but couldn't see the ground or the speed. If she jumped she could break a leg and be caught.

"Oh, dear," she sighed. She hauled the rope and the screaming whistle let out the last of the steam from the boiler.[53]

The train slowed and she could tell from the creaky clanks it was safe to jump. She stood on the edge of the footplate. She peered down at the ground. She bent her knees, ready to jump.

And that was when Locomotive No. 2 hit the buffers.

Instead of being thrown off the cab Nancy was thrown forward. Her forehead smashed into the regulator lever.

It had been dark in the park but it was darker in Nancy's cracked skull.

The boiler of Locomotive No. 2 split but there was so little steam it didn't explode.

The treasure coach jumped off the track,

---

53 It also frightened seven badgers, thirty-nine crows, sixteen rabbits and six hundred and thirty-two worms half to death. It woke seventeen hedgehogs from hibernation and made Lord Fumble's cook drop a plate of pies on the kitchen floor. Let this be a lesson to you. Don't go whistling in the dark, no matter what they say.

twisted and rolled on its side, jamming the door shut.

Locomotive No. 3 crept carefully along and stopped just before it reached the wreckage. If Nancy was a poor driver then Mr Rump wasn't.

The coal train stopped. Constable Liddle climbed down stiffly to the track and hobbled towards the wreck of Locomotive No. 2. Driver Rump pulled a lantern from the front of his locomotive and followed.

"We've got the treasure coach anyway," the guard said, standing beside the yellow, crumpled coach.

"No we haven't," Driver Rump said.

"Lord Fumble will want his treasure," Constable Liddle said tugging at the twisted door. "If it's not in here then where's it gone?"

"It was unloaded when the train stopped at the main road," Rump said.

"That man by the roadside with a pencil . . . he said they unloaded farm supplies," Liddle reminded him.

Rump shook his head. "That carriage wasn't *carrying* any farm supplies. We were so keen to catch this train we forgot that. They unloaded the treasure and by now they'll be in Wildpool hiding it. Lord Fumble won't see his fortune again."

"He won't be pleased," Liddle groaned. "Never mind. The Wildpool police always get their man. Let's arrest the driver and at least Inspector Beadle will be pleased."

The men walked along the track to the hissing Locomotive No. 2 and shone the lantern into the cab. Nancy lay there lifeless. "Yes, we have the thief."

"No," Rump said. "That's the fireman. The driver was an old man called Urnip ... he must have jumped off at the roadside."

"Ohhhh! I don't care!" Liddle moaned. "So long as Inspector Beadle and Lord Fumble have someone to send to Darlham Gaol they won't mind. Help me get the lad on to the coal train and we'll take him back to Wildpool Police Station."

And so it was curtains for Nancy.[54]

54 Curtains drop across the stage at the end of a show. Curtains mean "the end ". Which is strange, because in the Apollo Music Hall the curtains would soon be opening. As Smiff 's granny used to say, "As one curtain closes another one opens". You can see Smiff 's granny was a wise lady.

10 a.m. Tuesday 28th February 1837

In Wildpool Police Station there was joy the next morning. Inspector Beadle looked at his two officers. Liddle in his shredded uniform stood proudly in front of the station cell, a bandage wrapped round his burned bottom. Larch, rounder and redder and tidier, stood . . . almost as proud.

"The Wildpool police always get their man," Inspector Beadle said. "Except, in this case, it's not a man . . . it's a girl! Seems this Nancy posed as a boy to get a job on the railway."

The three men looked through the bars. Nancy sat quietly on the hard bench that served as a bed. A bandage round her head slipped over one eye. She did her best to look stupid.

"We know you were working with the driver," Inspector Beadle said. "The other driver, Rump – the one that trained you – says your friend's name was Urnip. Is that correct?"

"I think so," Nancy said.

"So this is who we are looking for," Constable Larch said and unrolled a poster.

"Is that picture a good likeness?" Beadle asked.

"I don't think so," Nancy lied. "I was just a trains-potter. Urnip asked me if I wanted to join him – learn to drive. Of course I said yes! But I always had the feeling the grey hair was a wig. I reckon he's about twenty years old."

Liddle and Larch groaned. "So we wouldn't spot him if we stood next to him in the tavern!" Larch sighed.

"Wouldn't spot who?" a quiet voice asked. The policemen swung round to see Lord Fumble standing in the doorway to the cells.

"This Urnip, my lord," Beadle said, showing the poster.

"Torture the prisoner. Get him to talk," the furious-faced Fumble spat.

"It's a girl, sir. She disguised herself as a boy to get a job on the footplate. She'd never met Urnip before."

"And you believe her, you idiot?" Lord

Fumble sneered. "I knew I'd seen that face before when I saw her on the platform at Fumble Hall. I said I knew the face. Didn't I?"

"Yes, Lord Fumble," Nancy whispered.

"It is the face I sentenced to forty years in Darlham Gaol. It is a Turnip face." He jabbed a fat finger at the girl. "You are one of the Turnip family, aren't you? Rick Turnip's granddaughter?"

"The granddaughter of his mother's brother," she said.

"And the driver?" Lord Fumble went on. "The real criminal mastermind behind this is your great-uncle, Rick Turnip. He was released from the gaol just a week ago and he's back to his old tricks. Isn't that true, you young villain?"

"No, Lord Fumble," Nancy said.

The lord shrugged his wide shoulders. "If we don't find the driver then you'll be the one to hang!"

Inspector Beadle was even larger than Lord Fumble and he rolled forward to block the lord's view of the cell. "Sorry, my lord, but the courts would never allow her to hang. They may transport her to Australia for seven years but no court would hang the child."

"The court will hang her if I am the judge," Fumble laughed. "And I am magistrate tomorrow. Have her brought before me." He swung round on the two constables. "And you two . . . go out and search every rat's nest between here and Darlham till you find Rick Turnip."

He stumped out of the police station and into his waiting carriage.

"You heard him," Inspector Beadle said to his constables and he turned and waddled down the stairs to his office.

Next door to the police station stood Master Crook's Crime Academy. The mood was of gloom . . . and rage.

Alice ripped the letter down from the noticeboard and waved it at Samuel Dreep, Smiff and Rick Turnip. "Have you seen this? Have you seen it?"

They nodded silently.

CRIME ACADEMY

To all students and staff.
As you know one of our new pupils, Nancy
Turnip, has been arrested while taking
part in the Great Train Robbery. This is
very sad and a lesson to us all. Nancy
was told to abandon the train after
the Fumble Fortune had been unloaded
at the Great North Road. Nancy chose
to disobey. She carried on and was
arrested. This puts the whole Academy in
danger.
    In future all plots made by Master
Crook must be obeyed to the letter. There
must be no attempt to rescue Nancy.
Plans to give away the Fumble Fortune
must go ahead.

M Crook

"What a RAT!" Alice screamed. "You
don't just abandon your mates! I'm going to

take this letter and stick it up Master Crook's crooked nose."

"If his nose is crooked you won't get the letter very far," Smiff said.

Alice glared at the boy. She blew down the message tube in the wall. "Are you there, Master Rat?" she shouted. There was no reply. She ran to the door that led to the cellar and clattered down, two steps at a time.

The heavy curtain hung there as lifeless as a hanged thief. She took a deep breath. She stepped forward. She pulled the curtain aside. There was a wide chair there. Behind the chair was a plain wooden door.

Alice tried the door handle. The door was locked. "Master Crook?" the girl shouted. "Are you there? Come on out. I want a word or two."

The only answer Alice got was silence.

6:00 p.m. Tuesday 28th February 1837

The poster outside the Apollo Music Hall was freshly pasted on and flapped in the chill evening wind . . .

APOLLO MUSIC HALL, WILDPOOL

SOLE LESSEE MR FARLAND

PRESENTS

TONIGHT'S PERFORMANCE CANCELLED

PRIVATE EVENT FOR WILDPOOL AND HELTON RAILWAY COMPANY

SHAREHOLDERS ONLY

PRESENT YOUR SHARE CERTIFICATE TO GAIN ENTRY

Customers who bought tickets for

THE TERRIFIC TORINOS' TALKING TURKEY ACT

will have their money refunded. Apologies for this short notice

Live in conversation

NO DOGS, NO DRINKING YOUR OWN DRINK, NO SPITTING AND LADIES ARE NOT ALLOWED TO SMOKE.

FOOD AND DRINK ARE SERVED AT THE INTERVALS, BEFORE AND AFTER THE SHOW

The heavy velvet curtains swung open. The drama began.

"Good evening, shareholders," Samuel Dreep cried from the stage. He stood behind a table. On the table rested lists of names. Treasure chests stood on the platform beside him with bags of coins inside. "I am Andrew Brown of the Fumble Estates," Dreep lied. He wore a gingery wig and eyeglasses to change the way he looked. But nothing could disguise the fine, fluttering fingers of the Crime Academy teacher.

Smiling Smiff and sulking Alice stood beside him, ready to help.

Some of the audience gave a patter of applause. Dreep raised his tall hat, bowed a little and went on. "Lord Fumble sent me to thank you for the faith you have shown in the great railway plan. . ."

"We don't want thanks, we want some money!" a woman shouted.

"I know," Dreep nodded. "It will be three years before the main line reaches this far north."

"Three years!" a man roared. "We'll have starved and be in our graves before then!"

Dreep held up his hands for silence. "Lord Fumble knows this . . . and this is why he has decided to pay a *dividend* from the money the railway is making."

"But last month he said the railway wasn't making money!" the woman cried.

"The coal trade from Helton Colliery to Wildpool river drops has done well. Lord Fumble thinks it is only fair that you should have a share. . ."

"How much?" the man called.

Dreep took a deep breath . . . a Dreep breath. "A thousand pounds," he said.

There was a moment of stunned silence then a ragged cheer, cries of excitement. It took ten minutes to die down. "You get this cash now . . . and you keep your share certificates. When the railway starts to pay in three years', time you will, of course, get regular money from it. Now, if you would like to line up my assistants will make sure everyone with a share gets their cash!"

Excited and happy people joined the queue and carried away their cash. Mrs Mixly clung to her husband's arm as he proudly showed his certificate . . . the last thing in their house. "It's roast beef and plum pudding for dinner tonight, my dears," she told the twins.

The last in line was a man with a scarf wrapped around his face. "And last, but not least," Samuel Dreep smiled, "we have your share, Andrew Brown."

"Hush!" the estate manager hissed. "No one must know how I helped you. Lord Fumble mustn't know I told you about his plans to move the treasure."

"You're a good man, Andrew. No one shall know."

Brown grinned. "And Lord Fumble wants no one to know he had that million pounds while the share-holders starved. It would make him unpopular – no one would trust him ever again. He wants people to think it was just about ten pounds in the chests."

"So, let the world think that," Dreep nodded.

"There's still money in the chest," Smiff pointed out.

Dreep nodded. "That will meet the costs of Master Crook's Crime Academy," the teacher said.

"But it won't meet the cost of Nancy's life if she hangs tomorrow, will it?" Alice spat. "All the money in the world won't pay for that."

The girl pulled her shawl around her shoulders and stormed off into the Wildpool winds that failed to cool the burning bitterness growing in her heart.

Chapter 12

FORTUNE
AND FAME

Wildpool Court – Wednesday 1st March 1837

Nancy stood quietly in the court, chained to the "dock".

The court was full with reporters. The first great train robbery would be worldwide news.

The clerk of the court was still the same fussy little man with spectacles and a bald head. But now he was eighty years old or more – ten years older than Lord Fumble. "Court will rise for the judge!"

Lord Fumble was dressed in the finest, scarlet judge's robes and a wig as wide as the doorway.[55]

His face wore a vicious smirk. Someone

---

55 Did you know, these wide wigs are called "Full-bottomed" wigs? Fat Lord Fumble had a full-bottomed wig and a full-bottomed bottom. A matching pair!

was going to suffer.

"What are the charges?"

"Highway robbery, I suppose, your honour," the clerk said. "It's hard to say. No one has ever robbed a train before. I'm not sure if there is a law against it."

"There is now," Fumble snarled. He glared at Nancy. "Do you plead guilty?"

A man in a short white wig and black gown jumped to his feet. "My client wishes to plead not guilty, your honour."

Fumble turned his red face towards him. "And who are you? And how can a gutter-girl like that afford a lawyer to defend her?"

"My name is Dreep, your honour," Samuel Dreep said, bowing. "Friends of the accused have paid for her defence."

Fumble leaned forward and said quietly in a soft but rasping voice for Dreep's ears only, "It will do her no good. No one steals my money and gets away with it."

Dreep bowed and smiled. "May I call a witness?"

"Call as many as you like. You are wasting

your time and mine."

"Call Constable Liddle of the Wildpool Police Force," Dreep said.

"Call Constable Liddle!" the little, bald clerk echoed.

Liddle stepped into the witness stand, took an oath and looked at the judge nervously.[56]

"You are a hero of the Wildpool Police Force," the judge said. "Get someone sent to prison for this dreadful crime and there may be a medal in it for you!"

"Thank you, sir," Liddle said.

"Constable," Dreep cut in before the judge could offer to pay the man a hundred pounds to lie. "Did you see Nancy Turnip take any money?"

"No, sir, but I did see her mess about with the carriage coupling."

"Did you see her pass treasure chests to friends at the Great North Road?"

"No, sir, but. . ."

"The treasure was loaded on to a cart on the evening of the robbery," Dreep said.

"We did see a cart drive away before we

56 You will be pleased to know Liddle was dressed in a new uniform and helmet. He had spent an hour shining his buttons.

reached the road. . ."

"But Nancy Turnip didn't go with it, did she?"

"No, sir, but. . ."

"Because Nancy Turnip is innocent. She was paid as a fireman on the locomotive. She did as she was told. The driver told her to stop, she stopped. The driver escaped and Nancy set off to finish the journey to Wishington Country Manor. She knew nothing about a robbery."

Constable Liddle shrugged his thin and rounded shoulders. "If you say so, sir."

Lord Fumble crashed a fist into the bench in front of him. "NOT if he says so!" he roared and his eyes were red with rage. "This girl is one of the evil Turnip family. The driver was her great-uncle – a man who has just been released after forty years in Darlham Gaol and who will go straight back there if I get my hands on him. Someone has to be punished for this crime!" He placed a black cap carelessly on his head and began to read the death sentence. . . "The court orders you to be taken from here to the place from where you came."

"Sorry, my lord," the old clerk said, "but you

cannot hang a child for stealing ten pounds. . ."

"It wasn't ten pounds it was . . . it was. . ." Lord Fumble stopped himself. He watched as the reporters held their pencils in the air, ready to write down what he said. "It . . . it was . . . ten pounds," he growled. "But I can sentence the girl to be transported, can't I? Just for being one of the Turnip clan she deserves that! Pass me a charge sheet. . ."

"My lord!" Dreep cried.

"Silence in court or I'll have you packed off with the girl."

Dreep buried his head in his hands, helpless.

In the gallery a girl struggled to rise to her feet but a boy with shaggy black hair held her down. "Not now, Alice . . . you'll get us all arrested."

SENTENCE RECORD

His majesty's judge	*Lord Justice Fumble*
Has sentenced on this day	*1 March 1837*
The criminal known as	*Nancy Turnip*
For the crime of	*highway Robbery*
The sentence being	*fourteen years' transportation*
Signed	*Fumble*

"Take her down," the judge ordered.

"The court will rise!" the bald clerk cried.

A figure dressed as an old woman in a shawl rose to its feet and threw back the shawl. "Wait!" the figure cried.

Lord Fumble peered at the figure and a slow smile spread across his fat lips. "Ahhh! My old friend Rick Turnip." The judge turned to Constable Liddle. "Arrest that man."

"Sorry, my worship, but me handcuffs are on the girl," Liddle said.

"Well . . . well . . . take them off the girl and get them on that thug!"

Liddle unlocked the handcuffs and moved towards Rick Turnip.

"Take one step and the girl gets it!" the highwayman cried. Under the shawl he pointed a finger at Alice White who was sitting next to him. "This pistol is loaded and I'm not afraid to use it," the old man said.

Alice had a brain as sharp as any needle. "Help! Oh, help! Don't let him shoot me, sir! I is as innocent as the day is short. I ain't done nothing to deserve to die young. I beg you, do as he says!"

"Wait!" Lord Fumble ordered Constable Liddle. He turned towards his old enemy Turnip. "If you shoot the girl you will hang this time. Put the gun down."

"Not till you set Nancy free."

Fumble raised his massive shoulders. "I will set Nancy free when I get the person that took the Fumble Fortune."

Rick Turnip lowered his finger. He took a deep breath. "That was me, your honour. I planned it all and I did the robbery. The girl trusted me because I am her great-uncle. But she knew nothing about it. Let her go. Take me instead."

Lord Fumble slowly raised the Sentence Record, crumpled it into a ball and threw it on the floor. He smiled at the newspaper reporters. "This is a great day for justice in this land! Lord Fumble has arrested one of the most famous highwaymen ever to plague our roads."

"Oh, thanks, your honour!" Rick Turnip blushed as Liddle snapped the handcuffs on the thin old wrists.

"This man is so cunning he even invented a new crime – a crime so new there is no punishment for it!" Lord Fumble roared on as a dozen pencils scratched away at a dozen notepads. "Where is my fortune? The Fumble Fortune?" he asked.

"The wheel fell off the getaway cart, my lord," Turnip sighed. "It rolled off Wildpool Bridge and sank to the bottom of the river. All ten pounds of it."

Lord Fumble gave his old enemy a look of pure poison. "So, Rick Turnip, terror of the trains, I hereby sentence you to. . ."

A hush fell over the court. A dozen pencils hung in the air over a dozen waiting sheets of paper.

"I sentence you to forty years in Darlham Gaol!"

A gasp ran around the court. Samuel Dreep jumped to his feet. "I object to the harshness. . ."

"It's all right," Rick Turnip said cheerfully. "I don't object. Take me away, Constable! I'm going home."

AFTERWORD

The rap on the Mixly door was heavy as an axe. Mrs Mixly skipped down the hall and threw open the door. "Mr Candy! Mr Knuckle! How nice to see you!" she cried. "Come in out of the cold and warm yourself by the fire," she said and led the way into the living room. A warm fire of coal and logs crackled in the grate. A fine stew full of best beef stood on the new table and two cheerful children were helping themselves.

Even the light was warm and butter-yellow from a crowd of candles.

Candy looked unsure. "We've come for the hundred pounds."

"We've spent a hundred on the new furniture to replace the old stuff you took away," Mrs

Mixly said and fluttered her eyes prettily at Knuckle. "But this new stuff is so much nicer, don't you think?"

"If you've spent the money we'll have to take something else. I did say we'd take the children and sell them to a chimney sweep," Knuckle said with a cruel smile. He grabbed Martin in one huge hand and Millie with the other.

"Wait," Mrs Mixly cried and she moved towards the kitchen door. She opened it carefully and stood there. "Are you saying that if I don't pay you one hundred pounds you will take my children away?"

"Exactly," Knuckle chuckled.

"Couldn't put it better myself," Candy agreed.

"I think that is called 'demanding money with menaces' and I think it is against the law, you naughty boys," Mrs Mixly said.

"Hah!" Candy sneered. "Like we care, eh, Knuckle?"

"Like we care," his partner agreed.

"But Inspector Beadle cares, don't you?" Mrs Mixly's voice trilled. "Don't you?"

The light from the kitchen was blocked by

a shadow as the huge form of Beadle loomed into view. "I care," Beadle said. "And I am arresting you. There'll be no more bringing misery to the poor."

Knuckle and Candy cringed like cowardly cats faced by bulldog Beadle.

"Oh, sir! We was only doing our job!" Candy cried.

"You didn't have to enjoy it so much," Beadle said. "Liddle? Larch!" The two constables appeared. "Take them away."

Rick Turnip's faded eyes glowed like jewels. He unwrapped the latest parcel from the Darlham book shop. The magazine was crinkly fresh and the old man stroked it with love. "What have you got there, my old friend?" the governor of Darlham Gaol asked.

"A new story by that young writer, Charles Dickens. His Pickwick Papers was wonderful, but this looks even better! *The Adventures of Oliver Twist – Or the Parish Boy's Progress. Part 1.* I think this young Dickens can become a great writer."

The governor chuckled. "You should know. I've never known anyone read as much as you, Rick!"

"Yes," the old man nodded looking at the sketches.

"It was quite nice in the outside world... I have a wonderful niece called Nancy ... a brave girl. She's promised to visit as often as she can. And the young people at the Crime Academy were great. But I missed my library."

The governor nodded. "And we've missed you. Now, I'm sorry to spoil your Oliver Twist treat but we've a couple of young men just arrived. They are really upset – sentenced to two years in here. They look pretty terrified, to be honest."

Turnip the Highwayman rose to his feet. "Leave them to me. We'll soon have them so busy they'll forget their misery. What are they called?"

"Candy and Knuckle," the governor said.

"I'll have them right as rain in no time," the old man promised.

They walked down the cold corridors together. "It's good to have you back, Rick."

"It's good to be home, governor."

In the gloom of the room below the Crime

Academy, Alice sat and faced the curtain. It moved as the door opened behind and the wide chair creaked as Master Crook sat in it.

"I'm not saying sorry," Alice said.

The sigh from behind the curtain was enough to make the walls tremble. "But I am saying sorry, Alice."

"What?"

"I was wrong. You were right. There is a copy of the Crime Academy school rules on the noticeboard upstairs. . ."

"I seen it."

"Add a new one to the bottom, Alice."

And that's what she did . . .

MASTER CROOK'S
CRIME ACADEMY

SCHOOL RULES

PUPILS MUST ...

1 RUN IN YE CORRIDORS AT ALL TIMES
2 BE LATE FOR YE LESSONS
3 DISOBEY YE TEACHERS

4 WRITE ON YE SCHOOL WALLS
5 SHOUT YE OUT ALOUD
6 CHEAT IN YE TESTS
7 EAT IN YE CLASS
8 PICK YE NOSE AND EAT YE IT
9 DAMAGE YE BOOKS OR CARVE YE NAMES ON YE DESKS.

BUT:
10 PUPILS MUST NOT PICK ON OTHER PUPILS. NO MATTER HOW
     WEEDY AND WORTHLESS A CLASSMATE LOOKS THEY ALL HAVE
     A PLACE AT MASTER CROOK'S.
     BE WARNED. BULLY NOT OR YE SHALL BE BULLIED.

11 *Pupils of Master Crook's Crime academy
     look out for one another.*

Lord Fumble sat in Wishington Country Manor. The room was decorated in hand-painted wallpaper with birds and trees, the curtains were rich velvet and the windows wide and bright. The ceilings were cream plaster, moulded to look like grapes, and the furniture was the richest in the land. It was like a fairy-tale palace of your dreams. But the old man was miserable. He didn't see the beauty. He only saw his empty treasure chest.

Driver Rump stood in front of his lordship and showed him a map. "There you are, my lord. The main line will be passing to the west of Wildpool in no time at all. We need to link up to it."

"I can't afford to build any more railway," the fat lord snarled.

"If you sell me the company then I will find people to put in the money ... but I won't cheat them the way you did," Rump said.

"I'll sell it for million pounds," Lord Fumble said.

Driver Rump turned to the young man by his side. "Well, Tarquin, what do you think?"

"I think he owes a million to the men who built the tracks and the stations – the people who made the three locomotives, Dad. And there's only one of them still running. The person who buys the railway will start out a million ponds in debt."

Rump shrugged. "See, your lordship? You owe a million pounds. The collectors will be knocking on your door and taking away your furniture soon. They may even have you locked in Darlham Gaol for debt."

"Not that!" his lordship groaned. "I'll sell! Pay me half a million."

Tarquin stepped forward and looked at the notepad in his hand. It was the notepad he used to collect locomotive numbers. "I've worked it out," he said. "The Wildpool and Helton Railway is worth . . . one pound. Sell it to us for one pound, Lord Fumble, or go to Darlham Gaol."

Lord Fumble looked in his empty treasure chest. Finally he spat, "Agreed."

Rump turned to his son. "There you are, lad! You own the biggest train set in the world!"

"A trains-potter's dream," Tarquin the trains-potter smiled.

Samuel Dreep answered the door. Mrs Mixly stood there with a twin in either hand.

"Master Crook?"

The young teacher spread his hands wide. "No. I am not Master Crook, but maybe I can help you?"

"The other day a girl from here was amazingly kind to us."

"That would be Alice," Dreep nodded.

"I would like my Millie and Martin to grow

up like that. I wonder if I can enrol them in the Crime Academy?" the woman asked.

"It would be a pleasure. All they have to do is fail a simple test."

"Fail? Most schools want you to pass."

"But this is not like most schools," Dreep said.

And that was the truth.[57]

28 February 1901

Ricky Turnip robbed the train
Highway robber, mighty brain
Ricky Turnip, poor and humble
Stole the fortune from Lord Fumble

Ricky Turnip is no good
Chop him up for fire wood
If the fire won't burn his head
Use his wooden arm instead.[58]

THE END

57 Outside my window the children are skipping. I don't suppose they know what the song is really about. But I do. And you do.

58 Yes, yes, I know . . . the last bit confuses Rick with the famous Tom Turnip. But Rick Turnip wouldn't mind that. In fact, he'd quite like it don't you think?